Short Stories

Volume 2

by

Thomas Ryan

Far and Wide
publishing

www.thomasryanwriter.com

Other books by Thomas Ryan
Short Stories
The Field of Blackbirds

New Zealand National Library
ISBN 978-0-473-31801-7

For Trevor and Rosina McGarry

Acknowledgements

I need to thank my long time writers' group who critiqued my work and helped guide me through the process of arranging my words into legible order, Trisha Hanifin, Sue Gee, Meemee Phipps, Karen Van Eden, Miles Hughes. Cover design is by selfpubbookcovers.com/RLSather. A must give a huge thank you for the assessment and guidance, bordering on mentoring, to Cate Hogan. www.catehogan.com . To Stephanie Dagg, from Edit-My-Book, for the proof editing and final polish.

Mostly, as always, I want to thank my long suffering wife Meg for her continuing support and who is owed such a debt of gratitude it would be impossible to repay.

Stories

Bedridden

Soft footfalls and the sound of cotton rubbing against cotton intrude into my thoughts. Navy blue fills the doorway then flashes across my eye line; recognition immediate, the familiar movements of my nurse. It must be 7.30. She always comes to my room around 7:30.

"How is my favourite patient today?"

She sings her words to me in the pleasant melodic tones to which I've grown accustomed. How does she expect me to be? I'm eighteen years old, I lie in bed all day and I don't go anywhere.

A check of the bedside monitor brings a nod. She takes up the clipboard hanging from a hook at the end of my bed and writes something on the chart. I wait. Her hair is different. It looks darker, shorter. She has been to the hairdresser again. That's twice in the last month. The pen goes in her pocket. She holds up the clipboard. Lines, graphs, scrawled notes, unreadable at that distance. I wish that just one time she would hold it closer.

As if reading my mind, "All's well," she says in a reassuring tone.

Sure, from her perspective everything is fucking honky dory. She's not the one with a smashed-up body.

A tick and the clipboard goes back on the hook.

Next, a check of the drip attachment taped onto my arm. Another nod of approval and now the part I look forward to every morning. She leans over to fluff my pillows. The perfume, it's new. An aroma I don't recognise. A gift from her boyfriend, or maybe she splashed out to impress a new guy. She hasn't said and why would she it's none of my business. Her breasts are so close to my face I could bite her nipples, then she pulls back, too damn quick for my liking. I need a reason to make her hover longer but I can't think of one. Now she has a brush in her hand. She's a sadist when it comes to my hair, and I want to yell at her, "Hey careful; you'll pull it all out." But I don't. It's her job. And I can't move my arms, can I? If she doesn't do it my mother will and I don't want my mother's breasts in my face.

The brush holding brown fibres wrenched from my scalp is dropped onto the bedside table, "Time to let the sunshine in, John," she says.

I hate sunlight. When she pulls back the curtains it's so bright it hurts my eyes. The nutritionist says I need the vitamin D or whatever the sun gives. There must be a tablet. Surely.

The room fills with light.

"There you go. That's much better. What a lovely summer's day."

She's always so chirpy. So chatty. I'd like to tell her how beautiful she is, and I will one day, but I have a problem. I've always been awkward around girls. Never know quite what to say. The longest relationship I've ever had with a woman is this one, patient and nurse. Does that count?

With Amanda, it's different. That's my nurse's name, *Amanda,* and I think I have a shot with her. She's relaxed around me. That's good, isn't it? Okay, I know she's a nurse and it's her job to be warm and fuzzy, but the way she looks at me, touches me, it's special - I'm certain of it. Yeah, okay, she's older than me, but not by much and at any rate I read magazines. Some women are into younger men.

Amanda's face reminds me of a film star, a leading lady. I can't quite remember the actress's name, but she is considered a beauty, like Amanda. Did I already say that? And Amanda is tall. I love tall women. Tall and slim is my perfect woman. Ahh, *who am I kidding,* any woman is my perfect woman.

For months now I've observed her - okay, ogled her - and studied every inch of her body. Her breasts are her best feature. Not too large, just enough.

Amanda checks my drip again then flashes a smile. "Bye John, see you later," and she is gone.

Another chance blown. Next time I'll make my move. Wooing her is at the top of my wish list but a girl like Amanda will have lots of boyfriends. And right now all I can do is daydream. It wouldn't be much of a date with Amanda sitting on the side of the bed sharing a bowl of jelly and custard on my hospital tray. No way. Best to not make any moves until I'm out of here. Sometimes I wonder that the accident might have been fate bringing Amanda and me together. I never believed in that nonsense before, but now I wonder. Stranger things happen.

I hear footsteps.

Three, no four pairs.

The doctors gather every morning regular as clockwork. Not a social gathering, more like I'm a new form of micro-organism on a glass slide. After peeks through the microscope they gather and whisper. Every so often a glance my way then back to the whispers. No one speaks to me and it pisses me off. I'm eighteen, old enough to understand medical terms for God's sake, so don't treat me like an imbecile. If the explanation was simply put I'd get it.

My mother can't be far away. She always comes in the mornings and always cries. I have no idea why. I'm alive, aren't I? The policeman said it's a miracle I survived. The smash the worst he'd ever seen. That's worth celebrating surely, but is she grateful? Not my mum.

4

Much of the day of the accident is lost to me. I remember my friend Raymond came by. Raymond and I met in junior school. Intellectually we were smarter than the other kids and I guess our waving arms answering questions the other kids weren't remotely interested in ended with us isolated like pariahs, and driven together by circumstance. Our competitiveness stopped at academia and never ventured into sports. The result was two disappointed fathers, but on balance, we gained two very proud mothers. I suppose we were geeks but neither of us gave much regard to the terminology. Why would we? We didn't care what anyone thought, we were having too much fun trying to outsmart each other.

Then, we discovered chess.

It offered a public arena for our intellectual battles. Our cleverness would be on display for all to see and Raymond and I relished the idea of it. We read every book ever published on the subject and played each other most afternoons and through the weekends. The bullies in the school, the jocks, tried to show Raymond and me up, make fools of us, but we ignored the jibes. Our mothers called them ignoramuses and pointed out that one day we would be icons, like Boris Spassky and Bobby Fischer, and heads of industry, while those assholes would be sweeping streets somewhere. I had no desire to be a head of industry but an icon sure as hell sounded exciting.

On accident day, Raymond came to my house. Both of us had made it to the semi-finals of the local chess competition, and if we won we would meet each other in the final. This did not concern us. From the start we didn't rate our opponents and had expected to win through anyway. It wasn't the first time for either of us. We had met many times in local and national competitions and often fought it out for the cup and a few dollars of prize money. The ratio of championship wins and losses between us was 50/50.

"Bath time," Amanda announces.

I hate bath time. The woman I love gets an eyeful of my privates and I haven't taken her to lunch. It's so degrading. What if I don't measure up down there? She's a nurse. She'll know what size and shape is best. I guess I'll know soon enough. When I ask her to lunch, if she looks at my crotch and turns away, the message will be clear, hi mini-mouse thanks but no thanks.

Life isn't fair.

I let her get on with it. Close my eyes and fight against getting an erection. Play a chess match in my head. But the titillating distraction of her new perfume is winning the day. What is it about perfume and women? They use aromas to trap a man like fishermen use bait to hook a fish but it's a waste of time in my opinion. Most guys I know would walk to the hook mouth open. Scent is an unnecessary enticement. We men are always on the verge of arousal, for God's sake. I should know. It's happening to me right now. I need to think of something else.

Girls did come to the tournaments. Mostly sisters forced to support their siblings. When it came to chess, Raymond and I knew all the moves. When it came to girls we were as lost as a blind man in a circle looking for a corner. The last time two girls smiled in our direction we debated what to do for so long they'd left before we came to a decision. We expected they might come again, to this tournament.

Raymond had a driver's licence but no car. I had no licence but my parents had gone away for the weekend so we borrowed my mother's car, a brand new Toyota. I could never imagine my parents giving me the use of a car let alone a brand new one, so there was no point in making contact and asking. My mother would be upset if she found out I'd taken her car but she would forgive my indiscretion. Luckily, in my mother's eyes I could do no wrong. At any rate, she would never find out so nothing to worry about. Raymond and I were the 'Chess Champs', at least that's how we saw ourselves, and if we were to have any chance at all with the girls, we needed to arrive at the tournament in style. If the girls showed up we would invite them to take a ride in the Toyota girl mobile.

###

"That's it," Amanda says and pulls the sheet up, the embarrassment over.

Recalling the accident has managed to divert my thoughts from my groin, enough anyway, to stop an erection. My eyes follow Amanda as she picks up the bowl and pours the contents into the basin by the toilet door. She comes back and gazes into my eyes. A warm smile with enough heat to match the sun, then she spins on her heel and leaves. Holy shit, there was something in that look, I'm sure of it. But what did it mean? Had I had an erection after all? I've never had one before but then I did lose concentration. She was telling me I'm a big boy, I'm sure of it. No doubt about it. I measure up. Cancel the coffee and lunch - that was a definite 'take me out to dinner' smile.

The chess tournament proceeded as expected and Raymond and I made it through to the final. Our opponents gathered round to congratulate us. We were all smiles. Okay, we might only be heroes to the local nerd society but a shake of hands and a pat on the back had Raymond and me standing tall.

The girls were back.

I saw them first and nudged Raymond. We had made the decision that if they came we would introduce ourselves. But now the time had come, confusion. One of us had to take the lead. We couldn't both talk at the same time. I took a pawn from the chess board and held it behind my back, passing it hand to hand. Then I held out two

8

clenched fists. Raymond picked correctly and won the right to make the approach, but then his legs turned to jelly. He wobbled as he stepped onto the stair. There were only three steps and Raymond missed the lot. At the bottom he was able to grasp onto the railing and stop his face smashing into the floor. In appearance he had managed to turn disaster into an athletic leap from the top step. It even gained a round of applause. While a traumatised Raymond puffed on his inhaler as he composed himself, one of the girls came over to me and asked if we would like to go with them to McDonalds after the final game. I nodded and she left.

The fastest game of chess ever played in a local tournament began.

I overheard someone asking how two incompetent chess players, such as us, made the finals. "The area standard is slipping," the whisperer muttered into the receptive ear. Raymond and I didn't care what anyone thought. We had girls. The Championship Cup had lost its appeal. In our immediate future, were girls, Big Macs, thick shakes and, if Lady Luck smiled on us, a nervous joining of hands.

This time the neurology specialist, Doctor Christian, leads the medics into my room.

"Good morning John?"

There are three new faces. Trainee doctors, at a guess, or whatever trainee doctors are called.

Interns? Two of them are female and pretty but not as pretty as Amanda. For the second time my genitalia are on display; more prodding and more poking. There should be a sign over the entrance of all hospitals; when you enter these doors leave your dignity behind. Dr Christian uses a pen to point out bits of my anatomy as if I were a diagram on a whiteboard. A few nods and mercifully the sheet is pulled to my chin.

They huddle at the end of the bed. A muffled discussion takes place that sounds like the buzz from a hive of bees. No head shaking. That's a relief. I get nervous when I see head shaking. Always a bad sign. One morning the patient in the bed beside me got a vigorous head shaking and an hour later his body was dumped onto a trolley and wheeled away.

"See you later, John," the specialist directs at me. The others wave and then they're gone.

My condition must be of enormous medical interest. I've overheard Amanda tell my mother that Doctor Christian is a leader in his field. I'm lucky to have him treat me. Apparently he especially asked the hospital board to allow him to be my doctor and monitor my condition. Lucky me. I suppose I should be grateful, and I am. I wish he would hurry his expertise along and get me the hell out of this place.

"Hi John."

It's Amanda. She sits on the bed.

"Your mother will be in soon. Another quick brush of your hair."

Mother. God forbid.

Raymond and I had agreed beforehand that we would play for a draw and share the trophy. Neither of us wanted to be a loser as it might affect which girl went with whom. Not that it really mattered. They were girls and that's all that counted. With the prize presentations over the girls introduced themselves as Beverly and Linda. Raymond's face revealed his life had breached a new frontier and I feared he would faint on the spot. I held onto his arm until he rallied and managed to move forward.

We proudly walked them to the car, hoping all eyes were upon us but when I looked back no one watched. No one else had left the hall. Our moment of triumph had gone unnoticed and brought on a short-lived sense of disappointment. That emotion was quickly replaced by an upcoming dilemma. Raymond and I experienced a moment of telepathy I would never have thought possible. *How do we split them up? What do we do?* Raymond flicked me a nervous glance. The girls, again, saved us from ourselves. They both climbed in the back.

At McDonalds there was no available booth. Thankfully the girls did what we had learned girls do: they excused themselves and went to the bathroom. Raymond and I scanned the restaurant. The only seating available was a round table. This is when our intellect came to the fore. If we sat next to each other, the girls would be forced to sit next to one of us and they again would be left with the responsibility of choosing. I secured the table and Raymond rushed off to buy the food.

Linda and Beverley returned. Raymond and I watched them without watching. Linda sat next to me and Beverley next to Raymond. Our plan had worked. We both wanted to scream out loud and throw our hands in the air, like when a striker scores a goal in football. Linda and Beverley were sixteen and chatty and giggly. We learned they came to the tournaments to support Linda's brother. He'd said that Raymond and I were the best. Raymond and I sat straighter, and over the next hour our nervousness waned and we came out of our shells as the girl's friendly banter relaxed us. We became talkative. Mostly about chess but surprisingly the girls didn't seem to be bored. Then Linda talked more and more to me, and Beverley moved closer to Raymond. I caught his eye. He was glowing. He had an aura. In McDonalds, amongst the French fries and Mexican sauce, we had played the greatest chess game ever.

The queens, checkmated.

Then panic.

The eating was over and now the time had come to make the long walk to the Toyota girl-mobile. We had managed to pair off at the table but what now? As we walked across the car park Raymond's shoulders tightened. He could barely swing his arms. I was no better and could feel my Big Mac trying to climb back up my oesophagus. Why were women so bloody complicated?

"There you are, all finished." Amanda stands. She steps back and holds up the mirror. "As handsome as ever."

She turns and places the small mirror on the table at the end of the room. With her back to me I appraise her body. It's the same body as yesterday but I never tired of looking at it. No fat lumps on Amanda. As she bends forward to drop a tissue in the basket I can see the outline of her panties through the material of her uniform. I wonder what colour they might be. White, I'm sure of it.

As we closed in on the car, Raymond and I ceased our jabber and went into shock. Our legs still moved but our minds had closed down. Our new-found telepathy kicked in again and we both dropped to tie shoe laces. The girls kept walking and stopped beside the front and rear doors. It was the first time I truly believed in God. Raymond opened the door for Beverley, and I for Linda. Linda slid into the seat and I climbed in after her. She hadn't moved right across, and when I pulled the door shut I pushed up against her. My arm brushed her arm. Skin touching skin. My heart pumped so fast that a bass drum and a thousand thundering hooves crashed through the top of my head. Raymond dropped the keys twice. In the end he had to drop his head and line up the key to the ignition slot, tongue flicking the side of his cheek like my grandmother's did when she was trying to thread a needle.

The girls giggled.

My arms had turned to lead. I wasn't able to help Raymond. There comes a time when a man must stand on his own. Then I broke into a grin. Raymond shot a look over the top of the seat grinning, as well. *Hell, man*, we were both screaming in silence, *we have girls in the Toyota girl-mobile. Who cares how long it takes to start the car.*

The monitor beside my bed makes a shrill sound. Within seconds Amanda is in the room. She throws me a quizzical glance and I'm thinking, *don't look at me - I don't know what's wrong with the bloody machine.* She presses the button above my head. A call for reinforcements. Then she turns her attention back to the monitor and fiddles with the knobs. The monitor is malfunctioning. Great, that's all I need. The doctors return. The looks thrown my way by the gathering crowd leaves little doubt that, as far as they're concerned, I'm responsible for the machine going haywire. Doctor Christian takes over from Amanda. He must know what he's doing because the shrilling stops.

"Close call," I hear him whisper.

What does that mean? What close call?

The doctors gather at the end of my bed in the now all-too-familiar huddle and mutter amongst

14

themselves. Amanda stands outside the inner circle, an eye on me and an ear directed toward the group. Finally the huddle breaks up and they leave the room. Not a crumb of information tossed my way. So much for keeping patients informed. Isn't there a law that says they have to? I swear an oath to myself that when I'm up and about, I'll lay a complaint with hospital management. It's not good enough.

I need a nap.

My mother will be here soon. I love my mother but I need energy to cope with her depressive manner.

###

Raymond sat in silence. Beverley tried to extract a sound from him, even trying a question about chess, but he had frozen. We had never been this far with a girl before and this initial journey had not been long enough to gain useful experience. Beverley looked across the top of the seat and caught my eye. I shrugged. I was pretty certain I could guess what had turned Raymond to stone. He was thinking. *Where to now?* We had the girls in the Toyota girl-mobile and now we needed a place to go.

Linda saved the day.

She suggested we go to the beach and listen to the waves and lie on the sand and watch the stars come out. As the car started I sent Linda a thank you look. Her hand grasped mine. Holy shit! My body frazzled as if it someone had shoved an

15

electrical cable into the side of my head. As Raymond turned out of the car park onto the main road, I heard a choir singing a chorus of hallelujah. Raymond was smiling, I was smiling, we were all goddamn smiling. Then huge bright lights screamed down on us like a shooting star and fireworks exploded in my head.

I've heard my mother discuss the accident with Amanda many times. They must have thought I was asleep or couldn't hear. The truck driver tearful, full of sorrow, had made a visit. He had wrung his hands as he paced, seeking absolution from my mother for crushing her son and her car. There had been nothing he could do, he'd pleaded. Raymond had reversed straight out in front of him. My mother told Amanda the driver had attended the funerals. Beverley's and Linda's families had refused to allow either my parents or Raymond's into the church. They blamed mine for rearing an irresponsible boy who would take a car without permission, and Raymond's for allowing their son to have a driver's licence.

How could they blame our parents, for goodness sakes? Stupid.

"Here's your mother, John." Amanda is giving me one of those meaningful smiles.

I wonder if my mother has noticed the connection developing between Amanda and me. She likes Amanda. They get on well, so no problem there if a relationship develops. Mum sits in the chair next to the bed. Christ she's crying already. This is going to be a long visit. To make matters worse Dr Christian and his gaggle of interns are back.

"Good morning Mrs Brownlee. How are you holding up?"

The specialist is being gentle with my mother. That's nice.

"I'm good. Thank you, doctor."

She obviously isn't okay but if she wants to pretend, fine.

"I see you made the decision and signed the papers."

Decision? What decision are they asking my mother to make? No one has discussed anything with me.

"Yes I have. It wasn't easy."

"Of course it wasn't. If it's any consolation, we almost lost John this morning. The monitor showed no activity for at least two minutes."

It was a malfunction, you moron.

"The machines are keeping him alive: he has no brain function. Rest assured, when we switch it off he will experience no pain. As you know, Mrs Brownlee, I considered John a special case and requested to oversee his treatment. I've ensured he has received the care he deserves but now there is nothing more to be done. I am so sorry. "

What the hell are you idiots talking about? I have plenty of brain function. I am not a vegetable. Mum! Don't listen.

"I will ask you one last time," Dr Christian said. "Do you agree to turn the life support machines off?"

"Yes. I agree."

"Very well, Mrs Brownlee."

Mum, what are you doing? I'm okay. Jesus.

"Amanda, why don't you take Mrs Brownlee to the cafeteria? The rest of you go as well. I'd like a few moments with John. "

Don't go, Mum. Don't believe him. Stay here. Look at me. Come back. I'm okay. I can hear everything. I understand.

"They've gone and now it's only you and me, John. I know you can hear me. I've always known. I'm a specialist. I've seen your brain activity register on the monitors."

What are you talking about? You've just told everyone I'm a vegetable. If I'm not, go and get them back, tell them.

"The girl in the car with you, Linda, was my younger sister. Your mother told me you're a decent young man, John. And I believe her. Under different circumstances we might be friends. But do you think it's right that you live and my sister and her friend are dead? Bloody unfair don't you think. After all, you are to blame."

No I'm not. I'm sorry, Doctor Christian. It wasn't my fault.

"My sister didn't die at the crash. She hung on for six hours. No coma like you, John. A broken body wracked with pain. So much suffering, and

18

that wasn't fair. Not fair at all. I won't turn off the machines today. I want you to suffer. I want you to know that any day now I will end your life. But not when."

Doctor Christian glances at the monitor. The heart rate races then slows.

"Good, you heard me. Until that day, John." He turns and walks to the door.

Doctor, please, don't do it. Please…

The end

Gerry

Wednesday night.

Gerry Saunders checked his watch: 7:15pm

In fifteen minutes the group would come through the door. Shoulders hunched, heads drooped, eyes down watchful of shoes that picked across imagined gaps in the floor. Then a mumbled greeting before they slumped onto their chairs. Nothing more would issue from this band of misfits without a prompt from Gerry.

He hated psychology. If not for the money, and a lack of alternative skills, he would have tossed it long ago. The cash made disagreeable encounters with his egocentric patients tolerable.

Just.

His eyes flicked around the office. He made no apologies for the Spartan furnishings; white walls, white ceiling, the only furniture his desk, a chair behind it and six other chairs lined up before it. The desk lacked family photos and on the wall were no framed medical degrees. Degrees would show that he'd started his career as a psychiatrist.

Psychiatry had not been for him. Dealing with the insane had threatened his own sanity. Depressed him. Prescribing drugs to blithering idiots to morph them into docile blithering idiots brought limited satisfaction. It reminded him of a recurring dream in which he endeavored to trudge out of a swamp with legs made of jelly.

The unpredictability of the delusional psychotic made him nervous especially when asking these grown men why they defecated in their beds and masturbated into the pages of library books. Give him schizophrenics any day.

When Gerry first raised the subject of a career change, his wife insisted he stay with psychiatry. Being married to a specialist had given Michelle a social status that her years of waiting tables had not. But Gerry said his decision was set in stone, his mind, unchangeable. It wasn't to be much of a change. When he analyzed his options psychiatry was all he knew and with these skills psychology the only alternate career open to him. It offered a change of environment and patient type. He could live with that. The day he downgraded to psychology Michelle became a hunter; armed with long shapely legs and a shock of red hair that would make an Irishman cry, she stalked his hospital corridors in search of a replacement husband. It did not take long. Within months she had run off with psychiatrist number two and most of Gerry's money.

Gerry's eyes dropped to his hand now splayed at rest on the desktop. His brow furrowed at the sight of his podgy fingers. Could he really blame her for leaving? Without the prestige of his position, what had he to offer? He detested his physique just as she probably did. In junior school he had been athletic and a scholar but with the onset of adolescence and the move to high school, he developed feelings of inadequacy and a fear of rejection. To compensate he became brash and rude to the point of bullying. He ogled women in the mistaken belief it made him sexy. Word spread amongst the female fraternity that Gerry Saunders was an odd and creepy young man.

To counter the isolation, Gerry became encased in a shell of indifference. He gave up sport and focused on his studies. The resulting loss of physical activities led to an expanding body, and the label of 'overweight nerd' added to his growing list of undesirable characteristics, making him even less attractive to women.

At medical school nothing had changed. He participated in mixed study groups and the female students were polite but never responsive to, "*Can I buy you a coffee?*"

Gerry sought solace in the arms of prostitutes.

He didn't care that he needed to pay for sex. For an hour he became the centre of attention of any woman of his choosing. The prostitutes pretended to find him entertaining and feigned enthusiasm for the stories he spun. The sex was always spectacular, and after faking orgasms they lay on their backs, panting, rubbing perspiration from their foreheads as they extolled his stallion-like prowess. And minutes before the hand on the clock above the door hit the hour mark, his lady for the night steered him from the room, but not before soliciting a promise from Gerry to return. He always promised he would and he always did.

Gerry could not have been happier.

For at least two nights every week, sometimes three, he became the man he always dreamed he could be.

It was after one of these interludes he first met his wife.

In search of a cold beer Gerry had made his way to one of the waterfront bars a few hundred meters from the brothel. When waitress Michelle sauntered between tables on the way to take his order, he imagined he was watching an angel. Her legs climbed forever before disappearing beneath a tiny leather skirt. Auburn hair bounced as she walked and lips pouted deepest red against milky white skin. She was tall and that excited him. In earlier years he would have found her intimidating but he'd developed a confidence from the sessions with his hookers. He openly studied her, and when he was certain he'd caught her attention he dropped his eyes to her chest. A small strawberry tattoo adorned the top of her left breast. His eyes lifted. Deep red lips broke into a smile. Gerry was smitten. He ordered a lager and then another.

He began to frequent the bar as often as he frequented his brothel.

Michelle agreed to a celebratory dinner when he passed his final exams. Over champagne Gerry told her of his plans. He wanted to practice psychiatry. It meant more study, but psychiatrists made good money. Michelle, a realist, concluded that Gerry would be a wealthy man someday and offered a better future than waterfront bars.

She seduced a more-than-willing Gerry into marriage.

He gave up hookers and turned his attention to his beautiful new wife.

Early into his new career, Gerry realized he had made a dreadful mistake: psychiatry was not for him. He explained to Michelle he would have to give it up. She turned on him like a viper protecting its nest. She had married a psychiatrist and he would goddam well stay a psychiatrist.

For the next ten years the thick, red hair framing Michelle's freckled face and highlighting her emerald green eyes was enough incentive to persevere with his miserable working existence. She demanded luxuries. He complied. But, like a wilting rose, the bloom faded, and once the petals had peeled away and rotted into mulch, Gerry's interest in Michelle fell into the same compost heap. Their relationship no longer held enough interest to keep him in a career that he had long despised.

When he turned forty, Gerry entered his office, packed his personal effects into a cardboard box and walked out of the building forever. He had had enough. Within a matter of weeks Michelle ran off with one of Gerry's colleagues and sued for half the marital property. He never married again. Hookers again filled his relationship gap. They kept him happy, never belittled him and the experience was always joyful and sexually satisfying. But he needed money to maintain his finance-driven relationships and to get the money he entered the world of psychology. The patients might be mundane compared to his earlier employment but they were closer to normal and listening to depressives complaining of broken marriages, dead-end jobs, sexual inadequacies and personality dysfunctions was a welcome respite from dribbling zombies.

The money left from the split of assets with Michelle was enough to buy two adjoining inner-city apartments. He installed connecting doors, lived in one and the other became his office. A good arrangement and living near the city centre meant as many hookers as his wallet could fund were within walking distance. Gerry needed money to feed his addiction and the easiest money came from group sessions. He organized as many as practicable.

Soft shuffles met his ears.

His evening group was gathering in the outer office.

Gerry stood and placed the six chairs in a half circle. He then pulled his high-backed leather chair from behind the desk and centred it. He intended being comfortable. The patients didn't matter and at any rate they didn't care. They often tended to walk about when they ranted. Gerry's lips tightened in a grim smile. It amused him that these people paid a hundred dollars an hour to vent their frustration on why they failed to achieve greatness. It surprised him that he'd found six with this particular problem and that they'd agreed to take part in group sessions.

He pulled six files from the cabinet and placed them on the table within easy reach of his chair, then placed a pad and pen on top of the files. He would make notes. Not because he had an interest in keeping records, but to prevent himself falling asleep. He was ready. He sat back in his chair.

A light tap.

Mousy brown curls poked around the end of the door. Gerry suppressed an impatient sigh.

"Hi doc."

Blerta always called him doc. Not doctor, as was his due, but doc. It aggravated him. He wasn't a cartoon character. He checked his watch.

"Hi Blerta. Tell the others to come in."

They entered, single file, mumbled, swapped seats. Gerry drummed his fingers on the desktop, betraying his irritation. He didn't caution his outward displays of impatience because no one in the group would notice.

Finally they settled.

"Okay. Who wants to start?" Gerry asked.

As expected Blerta raised her hand. She uncrossed the large dimpled legs, knees poking from beneath a crumpled green smock covered in yellow daisies. Gerry knew her to be twenty-four years old and he guessed she was twenty-four kilos overweight. Her breasts jiggled as she leant forward.

"Very well, Blerta. Off you go."

"My name is Blerta McKay. I'm twenty-four years old and I live at home with my mother and father. I'll go flatting soon." A pause, then a quickened pace. "But for the moment it suits. I'm single and that's my choice. I prefer my own company."

Gerry managed to hide a smirk. The only man interested in Blerta would be a whale hunter.

"When I finished school," Blerta continued, "I applied to an advertisement looking for models. My mother said I was pretty. I had photos taken and sent a portfolio out to agents. Two were interested and Mum and I went in to meet with them and decided we would sign with Barclays, the agency closest to home. In the modelling world they were very well known." Blerta glanced around the room. No nods of recognition. "Anyway, my career started: fashion shoots to begin with and then later magazines."

Gerry, along with everyone else in the room, had heard Blerta's story told the same way at every meeting. The others appeared to be listening and showing interest. That surprised him. All were egocentric. Maybe, like him, they were trying to solve the riddle of how an ugly fat girl could be deluded enough to believe she could become a model.

Blerta said, "After two years I had a reputation of sorts. The photographers liked me because they said the camera liked me. My agency sent my portfolio to New York. More photos were taken and I was offered a contract. It was beyond my wildest dream. I was on my way to becoming a super model."

Blerta suddenly stopped speaking. Without a word of explanation she slumped back into her chair and reached into her bag and pulled out a chocolate bar. The others looked from her to Gerry. Gerry shrugged.

"We can come back to Blerta. Who wants to go next?"

Later, in the brothel, as Gerry soaked in a spa bath waiting for his two-hundred-dollar per hour companion, he reflected on the earlier group session. The six had agreed to return the following week, which was a sign the meeting had gone better than expected. More meetings meant more for hookers. Blerta hadn't spoken again. Leonard had yelled and screamed and alarmed everyone with his failed footballer story. Maybelline whispered how she failed as a dancer because of big feet. Gerry mused that her feet did indeed appear to be over-generous. The girl could have gotten a job flattening bitumen.

Hudson had been the only group member to cry this night. Hudson, of similar physique to Gerry, had ambitions to become an international basketball player. Gerry had listened to the tale of woe with the reverence of a priest taking confession. Inside his head a voice screamed silent abuse at the absurdity of Hudson's ambition. Jackson was an actor with no presence, and Anthony a gay boxer who didn't like hurting his opponents. Gerry despised every single one of them. They were weak and he hated weakness.

The door swung open.

The sound and flash of light from the corridor snapped him out of his reverie. The door closed and the room again darkened.

The girl, early twenties, he guessed sauntered towards him. Her silk robe slid from her shoulders, silently falling into a crumpled heap on the floor.

"Hi Gerry, I'm Gracie."

The smile, forced. Too bright. Too professional to be real. Gerry's eyebrows drew together. He wanted his hookers to be good actresses. The management knew this. He had not seen Gracie before, she must be new. The other girls had not warned her. That was no excuse. And worse, the look of her, her youth and beauty: Michelle came to mind.

"Where's Jenny?" Gerry asked.

"She isn't working tonight."

"What about Crystal?"

"She's with another client."

"You can't be much older than twenty."

A rhetorical question.

He followed the line of her legs. Her thighs. Her crotch. Jesus. He had an erection.

Eyes holding Gerry's, Gracie reached behind and undid the clip to her bra. It fell away. A hot flush ran up Gerry's neck.

"This won't do. You're too young. I'm not a bloody pervert."

He had always been specific with the management. He wanted women his own age. They were his substitute for a failed marriage. He did not want a Michelle clone. He relaxed with older women, became less awkward. But Gerry's eyes stayed glued to the contour of Gracie's breasts. They were firm, not bouncy like Jenny's or Crystals. They looked unnatural. Like clay moulds. He tried to stop himself from staring but his eyes refused to budge.

"What's the matter, Gerry? You don't like these," Gracie said. She cupped her left breast and pushed it at him. Although the display had the attributes of wantonness he also detected a blush of shyness on her face. He was not to be fooled. He had been in psychiatry long enough to read body language. And he was reading that she disliked herself.

And she despised him.

Gerry had had patients like Gracie. They inflicted injury upon themselves, sometimes they even killed themselves. He looked for signs. When she spread her legs he saw the scars. Cigarette burns on the tops of her thighs. Old scars but still visible. It made him want to vomit.

Gerry's head was the only part of his body above water. He hoped the girl couldn't see his erection. His hands sank to cover it. She recognized the movement and set her gaze on his crotch and smiled. The heat in his neck spread to cheeks he knew were turning bright red.

Gracie's voice came to him as a whisper.

"It's my first night, Gerry."

She slipped out of her panties and tossed them back over her shoulder. Now naked she slow-danced. Her body gyrated to imagined music. Eyes glazed over. For a few seconds she was lost in another world.

Then she sat on the side of the spa, opened her legs.

"This shouldn't be happening, Gracie."

"You want me to leave, Gerry?"

The voice purred as she slid into the water. She moved towards him, and as she did so reached down and took his penis in her hand.

"At a guess, I think you're pleased to see me, Gerry."

"Let me be."

Gerry was immobile. He closed his eyes. Why wouldn't she go? Why was she doing this? She licked his ear. Oh God, the feelings. He was bad. He shouldn't let this happen. She was making him feel dirty. Why? Gracie moved into the bath and pulled his arms around her. *Jesus help me. This is not what I want.* He opened his eyes and looked into hers, snake's eyes, wide open and flashing messages. Was that torment he detected? Disgust? Hatred. There was no warmth. Not like with the other girls. These eyes could be Michelle's.

"You fucking slut. You bitch," he hissed through clenched teeth. "What are you doing to me?"

His hands stroked her throat. Softly at first, caressing, like holding a new born chick.

She laughed at him. "You're weak Gerry. Like all men."

Fingers tightened, harder and harder. She held his stare, "Be gentle with me, Gerry". But her eyes, they begged him to continue.

"You slut. You fucking slut. You deserve this. You should have left me alone."

He squeezed, his teeth grinding and his muscles taut as he forced her head under the water. She thrashed about. Clawed at him but he held firm. He held her under long after she stopped moving.

When he released her she stayed submerged.

The high-pitched scrape of a catch unlocked. A hinged panel placed in the metal door at head height dropped down, the opening wide enough

32

for a half dozen heads. The med students in white coats, clutching clipboards, peered in. The room that met their eyes was stark white. The only furniture in the room was a bed pushed up against the wall. On the floor a book lay open and a chubby naked man squatted in front of it, resting on his haunches, reading.

"Can everyone see the patient?" Doctor Steiner asked.

Five heads nodded.

"Gerry Saunders, a forty-two-year-old male. Mother, Gracie, worked as a prostitute, father unknown. Abused from age four by his step-father and institutionalized at sixteen. Gerry excelled at school. Good athlete, exceptional scholar. Socially an extrovert. This is unusual as most abuse victims become withdrawn. Gerry didn't. He kept it stored and instead threw himself into all sorts of activities, boxing, football, acting, but of course bottling up emotions can only last so long. One day at school he refused to participate in any more sports."

"He binged on chocolate bars, pies and whatever pastries were available in the bakeries he passed on the way home. Gained weight, of course. At this stage someone in the school system should have noticed but then teenagers are teenagers. Unpredictable. His teachers put it down to adolescence. No one cared. Everyone was too busy to notice. Gerry blamed his mother for his stepfather's abuse. One night while she was soaking in a bath he strangled her. Then he went upstairs and beat his father to death with his fists. As a young man Gerry was as solid as he looks now. We've diagnosed Gerry as psychotic with a well-developed set of delusions. We've counted six personalities so far. It's doubtful he will ever leave the hospital."

"Questions?" No raised hands. "Okay, let's move on shall we? Someone shut the panel."

The doctor turned and led his group to the next paneled door. A straggler student took another look at Gerry. He was now kneeling over the book, masturbating. She watched for a moment. Transfixed.

Gerry looked up. Smiled.

The student slammed the panel closed and slid the locking bolt across.

The end.

A Christmas Story

Once upon a time in Ponsonby - a sumptuous suburb nestled within the burgeoning metropolis of High Aspirations - lived a man of great expectations and finely tuned intuitions. His name, Lamar Holmes.

On a fine sunny morning, the type the people of Ponsonby expected to wake up to, Lamar Holmes walked along the tree-lined avenue and past the glittering store fronts to his favourite café, the Curds and Way.

A morning ritual.

For Holmes the day had not begun until he had consumed ground coffee beans from Columbia and a steaming morsel from the café's patisserie cabinet. When he pushed through the door a small bell announced his arrival. The aroma of coffee and freshly baked pastries wafted across the room, titillating his senses and triggering hunger pangs he had kept suppressed since waking. There was time enough for coffee, a hot blueberry muffin and a scan of his newspaper before his 8:30 appointment.

Holmes carefully picked his way across dampened tiles presenting a hazardous pathway to his usual table in front of the Christmas tree. Small lights flickered through dangling silver and red tinsel. He sniffed at a branch. The aroma of pine needles was not forthcoming.

"Plastic," Holmes spat in disgust, then glanced toward the waitress.

Mop in hand she stooped and thrust its raggedy head under the last table. Two sweeps and she straightened, stepped back and gave a nod of approval to a job well done. She picked up the bucket and disappeared into the kitchen.

Holmes removed a fibre of hair from the sleeve of his navy blue cashmere jacket then sat and spread his newspaper on the laminated table top. A soulful trumpet solo resonated from muffled speakers fastened to the wall behind him. The music was soothing and relaxing. No headline on the front page caught his attention and the next few pages similarly uninteresting.

His peripheral vision picked up movement outside.

A glance through the window, partially covered with the day's specials in bold lettering beneath renderings of green and white holly and red splotches representing berries, he spotted the lumbering form of Inspector Lou Stride. There was purpose to Lou Stride's demeanour. Holmes deduced his tranquillity was about to be intruded upon. Folding his paper he sighed at the inevitability of it and leaned back in his chair. The doorbell jingled and a shadow fell across the salt and pepper shakers. Holmes forced a welcoming smile.

"Inspector, may I offer you coffee?"

"No time for that, Holmes. I need your help. A matter most urgent."

"More urgent than coffee and muffins? I think not." Holmes studied the inspector. The grim features and jutting jaw he knew only too well; Lou Stride was not about to be put off. "Very well Inspector, out with it before you implode."

Stride placed his hands upon the table and leaned forward. Holmes found the movement distasteful; he was protective of his personal space.

"I have news of a deed most foul in the hamlet of Walking-Is-Worth-It. Kidnapping Holmes. All the town's children have gone missing and we police are at our wits' end. I need your deductive skills. Will you travel with me to Walking-Is-Worth-It?"

"This is where the kidnappings have taken place?"

Lou Stride nodded. "And right on Christmas. Stockings are full, Holmes. The families want their children home."

"Well then," Holmes stood.

The waitress walking towards him stopped midstride. She held a tray holding a muffin on a small plate and a long black coffee in a white porcelain cup. Annoyance changed to a, *you're welcome* smile when Holmes dropped a twenty-dollar bill on the table.

"Lead the way, Inspector."

The opening of a tunnel under the mountain at the end of the northern motorway had taken thirty-minutes off the trip to Walking-Is-Worth-It but Inspector Lou Stride had little respect for the efforts of city engineers. He sat hunched over the steering wheel guiding his twenty-year-old Mercedes at a pace well below the speed limit. Each car that sped past received a string of expletives from Lou Stride. Holmes, long used to the inspector's driving, turned his attention to the lush green countryside.

"Inspector, has there been a note from the kidnappers? A ransom demand, perhaps?" Holmes asked.

"No. Not as yet."

"Hmmm. Very puzzling indeed."

After an eternity the car slowed.

"We have arrived, Holmes," Lou Stride declared as he neared the cascading river that marked the town's northern border. Over the single-lane bridge and a snail's-crawl drive along Main Street, the inspector manoeuvred his Mercedes under the shade of a giant elm and stopped. The huge tree, behind a white picket fence and embedded in the grounds of a two-storey white colonial building, had been decorated with lights, coloured tinsel and baubles of various shapes and sizes; a more than worthy attempt at a Christmas tree, Holmes mused. A wooden sign hanging under the century old homestead's mailbox read *Hotel*.

Holmes perceived something amiss as he climbed out of the car: an emptiness of spirit, a sense of foreboding.

"Not many people about, inspector It's Christmas Eve and I would've expected to see the town centre bustling with last minute shoppers."

"Holmes, Christmas is about children. Shiny little faces opening gifts from under the Christmas tree. They are enraptured by the wonderment of it all. Without the children, where is the joy?"

Holmes smiled at Stride's frank display of sentimentality. He knew the police inspector had no family and spent Christmas on his own, but who was he to argue with Lou Stride's image of the most celebrated of days? There would be no merriment in the Holmes' household either.

Holmes followed Lou Stride across the street to the medical centre.

"The medical centre?" Holmes asked. "Why not the police station?"

"A witness to one of the abductions is undergoing treatment."

At reception a matronly woman dressed in white eyed both men suspiciously. It seemed there was no welcoming smile for strangers in Walking-is-Worth-it. The inspector asked to see the doctor in charge. The nurse picked up the phone and made a call.

"Doctor Carlita Watson is coming now," she said, placing the receiver back in the cradle.

"That's very quick," Lou Stride said, long accustomed to waiting in hospital halls.

"Efficiency is Carlita's way, Inspector."

A woman in her early thirties appeared through two swinging doors. She wore a white knee-length lab coat and had a stethoscope slung around her neck. She said something to the receptionist who directed her towards Holmes and Lou Stride.

"The doctor, I think," Holmes said.

"Really, Holmes? How can you tell?"

"The shoes. A woman as elegant as this would normally wear a cute black dress, hem just above the knee and heels that would lift her legs and show off her calves. If you look closely, she's wearing flats."

Lou Stride just shook his head in wonder.

"Good afternoon, gentlemen. I'm Doctor Watson. How can I help?"

Holmes quickly deduced that Doctor Carlita Watson's dazzling display of white teeth in a pocket of pouting red lips concealed a serious nature, and the silky unblemished skin of her oval face framed by short cropped black hair provided a fitting canvas for the pair of piercing blue eyes now studying the two men before her. The woman had

40

a beauty that Holmes knew would undermine the fortitude of a man weaker than himself. He made a mental note to be watchful of Doctor Watson. In fact, he might never take his eyes off her again.

"I'm Inspector Lou Stride and this is Mr Lamar Holmes, a consultant to the police department." Lou Stride said. "We are investigating the disappearance of the Walking-Is-Worth-It children. The woman who witnessed a kidnapping, can we talk with her?"

"She's resting now. You will need to come back in an hour."

Lou Stride hid his annoyance with a forced smile.

"I'm famished Inspector," Holmes said, "I missed breakfast, if you remember. Perhaps, if we need to wait, then I think lunch. Doctor Watson, can you recommend an establishment with a repast elevated above that of sludge?"

Lou Stride gave Holmes a stern look. He hoped the good doctor would not take offence at the casting of aspersions on local dining establishments.

"There is a restaurant on the river bank just before the bridge. You would have passed it on the way in. I'm sure it will more than meet your high standards, Mr Holmes."

"Would you care to join us, Doctor Watson?" Lou Stride asked.

"I wish I could, but there is much to do. The loss of the children has created an epidemic of hysteria and my staff have been overwhelmed with sedating frantic parents."

Holmes noticed Lou Stride tug uncomfortably at his tie. The anticipated pleasure of dining with the beautiful doctor had brightened his colleague's normally dour manner. Now, Lou Stride's head drooped like a sulking puppy. To Holmes' delight the inspector's hang dog expression had the desired effect.

The doctor caught the look and, with a hint of a smile cast a glance at the clock.

"Very well, I do need to eat, but I cannot dally," Watson insisted.

"We will be as quick as a wink," Lou Stride beamed.

The three sat at an outside table under an awning to protect them from the heat of the midday sun. The gentle gurgling of the river relaxed Holmes, as did the melodious tones of Dr Watson's voice whenever Lou Stride gave her a moment to speak. The besotted police inspector regaled Watson with exaggerated tales of previous adventures. Watson smiled politely and responded in the appropriate places, displaying a keen attentiveness that to onlookers would have seemed genuine. It encouraged Holmes to conclude that Watson would make a superb actress because Lou Stride was a terrible storyteller, having sent many a listener to sleep, including Holmes himself. He sipped his iced tea and remained silent.

"Holmes, many apologies for dominating the conversation. Is there anything you would like to add?"

"Nothing Inspector. You have related your anecdotes to Dr Watson with such eloquence that my input would only detract."

"Really, Mr Holmes?" Watson responded. "The Inspector has spoken so highly of you. Have you no praiseworthy comments to add in return?"

Watson's smile was mischievous, the sparkle in her eyes, playful.

"I've made some observations that I find interesting," Holmes said, changing the subject.

"You have?" Lou Stride looked about, perplexed.

"When we first entered the restaurant, the other patrons were watchful. At first I thought it was the normal 'stranger in a crowd' reaction, but now I'm not so certain."

Lou Stride looked behind him. They were indeed under scrutiny. He eyed a young couple two tables away and engaged them in a glaring competition. The couple turned away. Lou Stride could intimidate the boldest of men.

"You're right, Holmes. I sense an air of distrust and hostility. Why? And how could they know who we are so quickly?"

"This is a small town," Doctor Watson offered. "Gossip is as important as the county fair and pumpkin soup."

"But why the hostility? We're here to help."

"Kidnappers want ransoms. They know the police will want to obstruct the payments," Holmes said.

"Aha, I take your point."

"Look along the riverbank. What do you see?" Holmes asked.

Lou Stride shaded his eyes and stared. The odd piece of rubbish, a few broken bottles but otherwise a tidy, clean river bank."

"What about movement?"

"The river is moving. Is this what you are on about Holmes."

Holmes said, "Indeed not, Inspector. Look closely."

After a few minutes Lou Stride shook his head. "I don't see anything. Nothing at all."

"Precisely, Inspector. *Nothing* is the point. All that rubbish and mud but no rats. None at all. I stood on that bridge two months ago. They scurried everywhere. Interesting, don't you think?"

"Hmmm, if you say so, Holmes," Lou Stride replied, obviously not understanding the significance.

There was a commotion from within the restaurant. A waiter appeared in the doorway.

"Excuse me," he said, addressing Carlita Watson. "We need a doctor inside. An old lady is choking."

The three rose as one and followed the waiter. Doctor Watson knelt beside the old lady.

"Please, help me lift her."

Holmes and Lou Stride lifted the woman into a sitting position. Watson knelt behind her and performed the Heimlich manoeuvre. The red-faced old lady coughed out a spider. She looked up at Doctor Watson.

"Thank you so much. I swallowed a fly. Then I swallowed the spider to catch the fly because it wriggled and jiggled and tickled inside me."

Lou Stride congratulated the quick thinking Doctor Watson. Holmes noted the other diners stayed silent.

The distraught woman, her voice a notch above a whisper and barely audible, related her story.

"I'm a nanny to two of the children who have disappeared, a twelve-year-old boy and nine-year-old girl. They were playing in the backyard. I was in the kitchen making lunch but I could see them through the window. I needed to use the bathroom. I was only gone a few minutes. No time at all." She bowed her head, a nurse stroked her shoulder. "But when I came back, they were gone."

"Do you remember anything out of the ordinary before the children vanished?" Lou Stride asked.

The woman was thoughtful, shook her head, then paused, "The German tourist. A musician. He'd talked to them earlier, asking directions."

"May I ask how you knew this man was German and a musician?" intervened Holmes.

45

"Everyone in the village knows him. He got about. Very chatty he was and always friendly but, funnily enough not on this particular occasion. He seemed upset about something. His manner had frightened the children because they came running inside to tell me."

"And where could we find this man?" Holmes asked.

"Watering Heights. It is where Mr Johnston lives. He is the wealthiest man in town and the German is his guest."

Holmes said, "Inspector, I think we need to talk to this German tourist."

"I agree."

"I would like to come with you," Watson said. "If you do find the children they may be in need of medical assistance."

The unsealed country road wound its way into the hills, and as the trio drew closer to their destination, day turned to night. Unmoving clouds hung in the air. Streaks of forked lightning silhouetted the two-storey edifice that was Watering Heights.

"Interesting, Watering Heights has its own eco-system," Holmes said.

"It's creepy," Carlita Watson responded, then shuddered as a fingery chill massaged its way down the length of her spine.

Lou Stride put gum in his mouth. "What do you think, Holmes?"

"I think we need to be on our guard."

The branches of ancient trees canopied the driveway like lines of old soldiers reaching out and entwining their gnarled fingers. Lou Stride drove through the woody guard of honour and parked. A set of stone steps led to the entrance. Holmes pressed a red button under an ornate sign that instructed callers to do so. After a few minutes, the huge oak door creaked open.

A man dressed only in a black corset and stockings supported by pink suspenders stood in the doorway. A friendly welcoming smile spread across his heavily made-up face. With a flick of the head his long black hair swished to one side as he adopted a slinky pose.

"Well, hellooo there."

"Holmes, the man is a….," Lou Stride began, taking a step back.

"I'm the butler. Well, golly me. Fancy that. You must be a pooolice officer to be soooo observant. I'm from Transylvania, Trans for short, if you get my drift. Can I help you gentlemen?"

"We're looking for a German man," Lou Stride said.

"Fancy. *So am I*. Boom, boom! Don't you just love clichés? I'm afraid I have no idea where he is, but I do know he's not here."

"Then lead us to Mr Johnston," Holmes ordered.

"Top of the stairs deary," the butler said, then stepped aside. "Don't get lost."

"Unbelievable," Lou Stride muttered.

Holmes smiled but said nothing; police sensitivity training had had little impact on the discomfited inspector.

Rows of dead animal heads hung from the walls and beady eyes followed the trio as they ascended the staircase. Timber creaked with each step. Dim lighting added to the eerie atmosphere and Watson promptly placed herself between Holmes and Lou Stride as they reached the top of the stairs. An overpowering mustiness pervaded the upper floor causing Watson to gag.

Lou Stride led them through the first door.

A library. Shelves of books covered the walls, and in the farthest corner, behind a polished oak desk, sat Mr Johnston, head down perusing a parchment, a quill pen in his right hand. His bearded face looked up. Annoyance turning to naked hostility at finding his room filled with unwelcome guests.

"Mr Johnston, I am Inspector Lou Stride of the Great Aspirations police force. I'd like to ask a few questions."

Mr Johnston carefully placed the quill into the moulded silver inkwell.

"Ask away, Inspector, anything to help the police."

Holmes stood back, studying Mr Johnston. There was something familiar about his mannerisms, his look.

"We are looking for a German tourist. A musician. It is our understanding he is living in this house."

"You speak of Himmel Hamlin. Yes, he is my guest. But he is not here at the moment. Come back in a day or two?"

"I would like to see his room, Mr Johnston."

"I'm not certain I can allow that, inspector. A man deserves to have his privacy respected, does he not?"

"Now see here, Mr Johnston, my asking is a courtesy: I'm not seeking permission. Just point the way."

"I think we have a problem, Inspector," Holmes said stepping forward. "This man is not who he appears to be."

"Really, Holmes?"

"This man is my sworn enemy, Maurice Arty."

"By Jove Holmes how can you tell?"

"The beard almost fooled me but the scar beneath the right eye, I inflicted that the last time we met."

"And it won't happen again, Holmes."

Maurice Arty sprang from his chair and reached for one of the crossed sabres on the wall behind him. Holmes leapt across the desk and seized the other. He lunged at Maurice Arty but his arch enemy parried. The two men eyed each other, circling, waggling their blades.

"Where are the children?" Holmes demanded. "I have no doubt you are behind this foul deed."

"The children belong to me, Holmes. I have a contract signed by the mayor. Rid the town of rats and I am to be paid one million dollars. The payment was not forthcoming. The children are forfeit."

"I do not believe the mayor would sign such a document."

"Well, I do admit, the children part was in small print and in German - I have my friend Hamlin to thank for that." Maurice Arty laughed in an evil manner. "But it was signed all the same."

"Inspector! Take Watson and find Himmel Hamlin's room. I'll take care of Maurice Arty."

"Follow me, Doctor Watson, quickly!"

Watson looked anxiously towards Holmes. "Shouldn't we help Mr Holmes?"

"He can take care of himself," Lou Stride said as he strode off. Watson decided the inspector must know his friend better than she and followed after him.

"Holmes, at last I have the opportunity to exact revenge. You have destroyed too many of my criminal enterprises and now it is time to bring your interfering to an end." Maurice Arty swung his sword. Holmes easily dodged the razor-sharp steel. "Stay still, why don't you. Let your death be quick. You will suffer less this way. I offer a little humanity."

"You, sir, are a curse on humanity," Holmes said, as he parried another blow.

They continued to circle each other, sabre blade touching sabre blade. Chairs were tossed aside and then leapt over. Neither man gaining an advantage. Maurice Arty raised his sword and rushed forward, chopping down. Holmes blocked the blow then fell backwards feigning defeat. Maurice Arty raised his sword for the coup-de-grâce. Holmes swung his leg, catching his opponent on the knee. As Maurice Arty bent in pain, Holmes swung his sword and sent Maurice Arty's sabre scything through the air. It sliced through a portrait of Maurice Arty's mother and embedded itself into the wall.

Holmes scrambled to his feet, the duel over. Maurice Arty stepped backwards into the far right corner of the room. Holmes smiled: his old adversary was trapped. Then Maurice Arty reached down and pulled on a lever. A panel in the wall opened and he disappeared through the panel closing behind him. Cursing the scoundrel's trickery, Holmes tried to follow but the secret door would not open. A lock on the other side, he surmised.

"He escaped," Holmes said in answer to the quizzical looks from Lou Stride and Watson as he entered Hamlin's room.

"Jolly bad show. Next time you will have him, I'm sure of it," Lou Stride said.

Watson's consoling smile morphed into a heartening display of relief that he had returned unharmed. Holmes noted the sentiment. A genuine surprise that a beauty such as Carlita Watson might fear for his safety.

Lou Stride held up a long hollowed-out reed and a collection of colourful clothes. "Tell me, Holmes, I'm mystified. What do *you* make of this?"

Holmes examined the tube and clothes and nodded knowingly. "It is just as I suspected, Inspector. I have seen this tube before. It is a pipe. Now, I wonder if I can remember some of the tunes."

Holmes scratched his forehead, a habit when thinking. Then he began to play. Watson and Lou Stride were an appreciative audience to Holmes' musical talent. After a few minutes, Holmes stopped.

"A pretty tune," Lou Stride said. "But what does it all mean...?" He paused, listening. "Hold on. Do you hear that? What can it be?"

All round, in the walls, the ceiling, the corridors, came scratching sounds.

"Nothing that will delight us, I'm afraid. We must leave. Quickly! Follow me."

They rushed into the hallway, but it was too late. Rats were coming from everywhere.

"Back inside and bolt the doors!"

"What now? We can't hold them off forever," Lou Stride yelled.

Watson opened her mouth but a scream was not forthcoming. Holmes was grateful. He disliked it when women screamed. She truly was a woman of substance, no doubt about it.

"I remember another tune," Holmes said, again bringing the pipe to his lips.

This time the notes were piercing. Watson covered her ears.

After a few minutes the scratching subsided. Holmes dropped the pipe away from his lips. Silence. Then the sound of high heels stepping along the varnished wood floor of the hallway. The footsteps stopped outside the door. Watson moved closer to Holmes. She clutched at his arm.

Lou Stride reached forward and pulled the door open.

"*There* you are," the transvestite butler said. "That was a really nasty experience. I was up to my knickers in rats."

"Your master has gone. Where is Himmel Hamlin?" Holmes asked.

"When it comes to Germans, I know nothing."

"What now, Holmes?" Lou Stride asked. "You seem to know this German. Who is he?"

"He is known as Pied Piper Hamlin, an infamous ratter and child kidnapper. Find Himmel and the children will not be far. Does this house have a basement?" Holmes asked the butler.

"A dungeon, no less," the butler said proudly. "Lots of chains and shackles. Very kinky. Follow me."

###

Halfway down the stairwell the shrill tones of a pipe could be heard from below. Holmes looked behind and saw the transvestite butler was not following.

"Holmes, that sound must be Himmel Hamlin," Lou Stride whispered.

"Yes. He must be preparing to take the children through a secret tunnel."

"A secret tunnel?"

"Maurice Arty has never lived in a house that did *not* have secret passages. We must hurry."

The corridor at the bottom of the stair led into an underground cavern.

Under an hypnotic spell woven by the soulless music, children were pouring out of dungeons chiselled into the cavern walls. They were following Himmel Hamlin to whatever dastardly meanness awaited them.

When Himmel saw the trio he stopped playing and shoved his mauve pipe into the top of his trousers to free his hands in readiness for Holmes's onslaught. Holmes did not disappoint. He rushed forward to grab hold of Himmel's colourful tunic and swung him against one of the dungeon's doors. Himmel let out an anguished cry. Staggering to one side, he reached behind a wooden pillar to pick up an iron bar – conveniently placed there for such a purpose – and swung. Holmes was ready and moved under it. The force of the swing threw Himmel off-balance and Holmes seized the opportunity, plucking away Piper Himmel's purple pipe, putting paid to his piping pursuits. Himmel tried to rush past, but Holmes was too quick for him and plunged the pipe through Himmel's palm, pinning him to a painted pole.

"Holmes! Are you all right?" Lou Stride yelled.

I'm fine, Inspector. Himmel tried to get away but I piped him at the post."

"Let's get these children back to their worried parents," Lou Stride said. "Alas, it is the end of another adventure."

"Have no fear, Inspector there will be many more.

The townsfolk gathered under the giant elm tree to celebrate the return of the children. Watson stood between Holmes and Lou Stride as the three heroes drank hot toddies and, along with the rest of the crowd, soaked up the Christmas atmosphere of the flashing lights and tinsel and assorted metal objects used in the tree's decoration.

"What sort of tree is that?" Watson asked Holmes.

"It's an element-tree, my dear Watson."

"Very funny, Holmes," Lou Stride said and laughed.

Then he and Holmes exchanged un-Christmas like glances across the top of a joyous and unsuspecting Watson.

"Merry Christmas, everyone," the Mayor cried, lifting up his mug.

"Merry Christmas," the crowd yelled back and then broke into a verse of 'The Red Baron' and they all lived happily ever after except for Holmes and Lou Stride who jostled for Carlita Watson's attention the whole night through.

The end

John Wayne

The silver Nissan came to an abrupt stop, the momentum flinging Sophie forward. As the seat belt cut into her breasts she stifled a gasp, gave a quick glare at David then made an equally rapid turn away and a clench of teeth. He had hurt her but she was not about to let on. When he sulked he was unpredictable, and if he sniped at her right now she would cry. If he apologized and tried to comfort her, she wasn't certain she would stay mad at him and she wanted to stay mad. He was her boss of sorts and that pissed her off. It left her with few choices. She needed her job, and to keep it she had to keep her mouth shut. Nowadays journalism was a tough business. Newspapers closed down daily and *The Evening Star* was one of the few still employing reporters.

The biggest mistake she had made was climbing into bed with him.

Now they were on an assignment together and the night had not started well.

Sophie had suggested to her editor that a series of interviews with old soldiers might be a good idea. The centenary of the First World War would keep stories of any war since 1914 in the public interest domain for at least the next four years. The Returned Services Associations were filled with veterans ready to talk of their experiences and too many stories were being lost as old soldiers went to their final last post.

The editor had agreed but insisted that David, as senior journalist, should oversee the articles. Sophie had not argued. The editor was fair. Sophie's name would appear in the byline. What had upset her most was that David had not wanted to do the articles. When she first raised it with him he scoffed.

David turned the key and the motor died; he sat, eyes fixed on a spot on the window, his breathing heavy in the silence. Without looking she knew his bottom lip would have drooped. He would be pouting, a common sight lately when he couldn't get his own way. Tonight they were on their way to an RSA to talk to a few old soldiers and set up interview times. David insisted he drive. Sophie accepted but with reservations. He would ply her with drinks at the servicemen's club in the belief her defenses would weaken and she would open her legs. Fat chance. She would catch a taxi home. However, her acceptance of his driving included a proviso they call in to check on her grandfather. Her mother had insisted and it was on their way. Now they were at her grandfather's she sensed David was already conniving on how to make an early exit, but she would stay as long as it took and David be damned.

He pulled the key from the ignition then sat back in his seat jiggling the key ring between his fingers. Sophie released the seatbelt and rubbed her chest. She should never have agreed to drive with him. The David she first met was a caring, attentive and sensitive man. Then they had sex and he changed. How naïve and stupid she had been. A workplace romance had risks but David being nothing more than a womanizer had never occurred to her, and now the stress of seeing David daily and holding onto her job had her scratching her arms most nights - a nervous habit from childhood. And here they were at her grandfather's and her arm itched like hell.

"Are you coming in?" Sophie asked.

"We're late, Sophie. You run in. I'll wait here."

"Would it kill you to say a quick hello? You've met Granddad before, and it will hurt his feelings knowing you wouldn't come in."

"Don't tell him."

"I'm not lying to my grandfather."

David firmed his chin. "All right. But in and out! Okay?"

He flung open the door, climbed out then stomped past the front of the car and onto the footpath. He waited with his back to her. She toyed with the idea of staying put then decided against it.

Instead, she climbed out of the car, slammed the door shut and stormed past. David aimed his key at the car and pressed the lock button. By the time he made the veranda Sophie had knocked twice.

"He could be asleep," David whispered, hopeful.

Sophie ignored him and tried the handle. The door opened. She stepped inside.

"Granddad," she yelled. "It's me, Sophie." To David she said, "He'll be in the lounge, crashed in front of the television." She made her way along the hallway leaving David standing the doorway. "There you are."

"Sophie," Andrew Johnson said, a little confused. "What are you doing here? Is it my birthday?"

"No Granddad, it's not your birthday. Mum asked me to check in on you. She worries. You left the front door unlocked again."

He gave her a sheepish grin.

"What are you watching?" She picked up the DVD cover. "John Wayne again. There are other DVDs."

"John Wayne will do me fine," he replied. A grumpiness to his tone. "And I don't need you mothering me. Your mother is bad enough. Why aren't you at a party somewhere? It is Friday night, isn't it?"

"I'm working. I have a colleague with me. You remember David Jensen?" Andrew nodded that he did. "He's waiting outside," Sophie smiled. "We're working on an assignment together."

"Invite him in."

Sophie stepped into the hall and waved to David still standing in the doorway. He glared but moved forward and followed her into the sitting room.

David waved. Andrew Johnson waved back.

"How do you do, sir?"

"Can I make you some tea? Have you eaten?" Sophie asked.

"I might be almost ninety, but I'm not an invalid. What work are you doing on a Friday night? You're still doing that silly journalism. Give it up. There is no future in it. I told you this before."

"Granddad worked as a reporter many years ago," Sophie said to David. "For real newspapers that employed objective, dogged journalists who pounded pavements seeking the truth and not downloading news stories off the internet. Isn't that right, Granddad?"

"Mock all you want young lady, but in the good old days a reporter had respect. We had ethics. We didn't manufacture stories just to sell newspapers. Not like today."

David said nothing. Looked at his watch.

Sophie kissed her grandfather on the cheek. He softened.

"And what is your assignment?"

"We're doing a series of war stories. We need to interview a few old soldiers and thought the RSA would be a good place to start. We're on our way there now."

Andrew nodded.

"And what type of story is going to grab your attention?"

Sophie shrugged, "I guess we do the interviews and then decide what might interest our readers. It would be exciting to find a juicy untold story but I doubt very few secrets of the Second World War, Korea and even Vietnam are yet to be told. David thinks all we'll get to hear will be exaggerated anecdotes; nothing of any substance. But that's okay, personal stories of everyday life in combat will still appeal to our readers."

David's lips curled into a half smile, eyebrows raised into twin arches.

"You might have the makings of a real journo after all. Your friend seems destined for the tabloids," Andrew said, springing to his grand-daughter's defence.

"I see you're a fan of John Wayne," David said ignoring the comment.

"You've heard of John Wayne?"

"My grandfather was a fan. I can't say I've seen any of his movies. Too slow and corny to have any real interest today, I should think."

Sophie glared. "Granddad has them all. I've been watching them with him since I was a child.

Red River is our favourite, isn't it Granddad? Or at least I think it is. That's the one we always watch."

"John Wayne was a great man," Andrew said.

"With all due respect Mr Johnston, an actor hardly classifies as a great man."

Andrew Johnson nodded. Thoughtful. He pointed to the book case.

"Sophie, pass me that scrapbook on the bottom shelf."

David caught Sophie's eye as she moved forward and gave her a 'we've got to get the hell out of here' look. Sophie retrieved the scrapbook and placed it on her grandfather's lap then sat beside him. He flicked through the yellowing pages, cuttings of newsprint taped to each leaf.

"Aha, here it is."

He put his finger on the headline.

"Doctors have confined President Roosevelt to bed for one week," Sophie read the headline out loud. "The President has flu. I'm sorry Granddad, but what has this to do with John Wayne?" She paused and leaned closer reading the date at the top of the page, "On April 27th 1942."

"Because, my dear granddaughter," Andrew Johnson said, a twinkle in his eye. "Roosevelt never had the flu. In fact, that week he wasn't even in the USA and nor was John Wayne."

"In 1942 I was a major, assigned to MacArthur's staff in the Philippines. That's General Douglas MacArthur of World War II fame. I'm picking even you two have heard of him."

Sophie and David nodded. Sophie's eyes narrowed, a hint of a frown.

"You've never mentioned you were in the war before, Granddad."

A smile from Andrew. "I had no desire to talk of those years, but now, why not? Japanese forces surrounded our defenses in Bataan," he continued. "The supply lines cut, munitions running out, our troops faced a hopeless task. Can't fight without bullets. The mood in HQ was grim: without a miracle the army, thousands of men, would be lost to the enemy.

"The President ordered MacArthur to be evacuated. At first McArthur refused but did move his headquarters and family to Corregidor Island. But the Japanese could not be stopped. In the end the President was insistent and ordered a submarine be sent. MacArthur rejected that plan and decided instead to bust through the Japanese blockade in PT Boats. At sunset his family and staff, including me, boarded the vessels and for two days we crashed through the rough seas until we made it to Cagayan on Mindanao Island. From there a B-17 Flying Fortress flew us to Australia. The decision to leave made all of us sick in the stomach. To leave men behind on the field of a battle is not what a military officer is trained to do. It stayed with me the rest of my life. For MacArthur, it was the harshest decision of his career. The closest I had ever seen this tough, military man come to shedding a tear. But he had no choice. He was commander of the Allied Forces in Southeast Asia and one of the US's leading commanders. He could not be captured by the Japanese.

"On the dock, as we boarded the evacuation craft, MacArthur vowed to return and of course he did. Two days after arriving in Sydney, before I'd had time to wipe the Philippines mud and sweat from the pores of my skin, MacArthur called me to his office. I was unfamiliar with the Aussie barracks and arrived a few minutes late. I tapped on the door and entered.

"'General. You sent for me.'

"MacArthur, pissed off with life in general, was in no mood for tardy officers.

"'I expected you half an hour ago Andrew.'

"'Yes sir. My apologies,' I said.

"I did not offer an excuse. He needed a whipping boy and I would have to live with it.

"'Take a seat.'" MacArthur pulled out his pipe and indicated for me to light up if I wished. I tapped a Kensington out of the crushed packet from my tunic pocket and lit up from the match offered. "'I have orders for you. Not happy with them. No sir, not happy at all.'

"I nodded and sucked in some nicotine.

"'You're to fly to the USA, Andrew. You leave in three hours. Select six men to take with you.

This is a security duty. Select men who can look after themselves,' he told me.

"'May I ask the nature of the assignment?' I said.

"'You may, but I can't tell you. All very hush, hush and even I, the man most responsible for stopping this bloody war, is not being let in on the secret. So no, I can't tell you anything. You land at Los Angeles. You walk across the tarmac to a waiting plane and board it. That's it,' he said.

"'Someone is flying seven soldiers from Australia to Los Angeles just to change planes,' I asked, incredulous.

"'That's it, Andrew,' he replied. 'Now I suggest you get moving.'

"I stood and gave a salute and by the time I had reached the door MacArthur was already reading another document."

"The trip from Sydney to Los Angeles took thirty hours because we couldn't fly direct. Japanese planes patrolled the Pacific and the range of the C-46 Commando was less than three hundred miles. A fifty-seater with limited leg room. Not like modern planes. But with no other passengers we had room enough to stretch out and catch up on sleep.

"We bunny-hopped all the way. Brisbane, the Marshall Islands, Hawaii and onto Los Angeles. We arrived exhausted. I needed a shower and to collapse into a comfy bed. The welcoming committee standing on the tarmac had other ideas.

"'Major Johnston welcome to LA,' the colonel waiting for us said.

"I shook the offered hand.

"'Thank you, Colonel. We need to clean up,' I said.

"'Sorry Major, there's no time. You're leaving right away.'

"'What are my orders, Colonel?' I asked.

"'You get on that plane yonder. Where the plane is going, I can't tell you. Pick up your kitbags and follow me,' was the response.

"My men made no attempt to stifle disgruntled sighs as we ambled across to another C-46. I had lost track of the time and it was dark and raining. We boarded in drenched clothing. An airman stowed our kitbags and handed out towels. A curtain separated the front of the cabin from the rear. My men were told that beyond the curtain was out of bounds, except for me. My orders were to proceed to the rear of the plane once I had dried myself off.

"I toweled my hair and attempted to flatten it down with my hand. A quick touch of my face told me I needed a shave. Well, that wasn't going to happen. When I stood before the curtain I hesitated. My appearance, shabby at best, would never pass muster. The military never accepted excuses for a poor turnout even in wartime. I hoped whoever waited on the other side would cut me some slack.

"I took a deep breath and stepped through the curtains.

"Four sets of eyes fell upon me and the faces shone with mild amusement at my open-mouthed astonishment. In a wheelchair at the rear sat President Theodore Roosevelt. Seats had been removed down either side of the centre aisle. Behind Roosevelt was a woman in her twenties dressed in a naval uniform. Seated in the first row a four-star general, and behind him a face I recognized immediately. I had seen enough of his movies.

"It was John Wayne.

"'Come on in son,' Roosevelt said. 'Make yourself comfortable. Mandy, mix the major a drink. You do drink, don't you, Major?' I nodded. 'Make it whiskey, Mandy. The major looks as if he needs warming up.'

"Speechless, I sat. Roosevelt produced a cigar, clipped off the end and twirled it in his mouth, then lit up. Mandy passed me a glass of whiskey and then returned to her position behind the President.

"'Let me introduce the team here,' Roosevelt continued. 'Mandy is my assistant. Gets me what I need most of the time but has the help of a doctor, a nurse and a couple of strapping marines who get to carry me everywhere. For the purposes of this get-together I had to leave them behind. Your men get the pleasure of toting your President about. General Beazley here, is Chairman of the Joint Chiefs and I must say, on his behalf, he was anti my taking this trip. Last, a man I'm sure you recognize, Mr John Wayne. I will be forever grateful to Mr Wayne. His President called him to service and he obliged.'

"Wayne nodded in my direction.

"'You must be wondering why you're here,' said Roosevelt. 'All I can tell you for now is that, you and your men are to protect me and we are headed for Argentina. Get me there and back alive and you will have done your country a great service. Now, down your whiskey, Major, and buckle up. You're about to take a flight into history.'

###

"Granddad, you're pulling my leg!"

Sophie looked across at David as she poured tea for everyone. He no longer wrung his hands. A sure sign the story for the moment held his interest. She hoped it would last.

"Why have you never mentioned you met John Wayne?"

"Not at liberty to, Sophie. Official secrets, and all that stuff."

"What happened next, Mr Johnston?"

"A long flight David. Another long, long flight."

###

"I had never been to Argentina but in those days Buenos Aries was the Paris of South America. A bustling metropolis inhabited by millions and filled with cafés, restaurants, theatres, movie houses and expensive shopping. Somewhere your grandmother would have loved to visit.

"When we landed, the C46 taxied toward a line of trucks and buses standing on the tarmac. In front of the vehicles it appeared the entire Argentine Army had turned out. I smiled and shook my head. Security was not going to be an issue. My men and I would be no more than presidential nurse maids. When the plane came to a stop I left my men to help offload Roosevelt and I disembarked.

"The Commander of the Argentine marines saluted then introduced himself as Colonel Juan Peron."

"No way!" David almost jumped out of his chair. "Juan Peron. The, *Evita*, Juan Peron?"

"One and the same, but of course he wasn't yet president and he hadn't met Eva."

"You are shitting us, Mr Johnston. Sorry, messing with us."

"I assure you that everything I'm telling you is how it happened."

Sophie caught David's eye and saw the skepticism. She gave a slow shake of the head. A warning to David to keep his mouth shut. She loved her grandfather. Let him tell his story, and even if it was fantastical what did it matter? David fell back into his seat. She touched her grandfather's shoulder.

"Then what, Granddad?"

"The buses transported us to the Alvear Palace Hotel; the most beautiful hotel in all of Buenos Aries and, in fact, the world. On the outside the architecture was grand and inside as majestic as any French palace. Crystal chandeliers hung from the ceiling and the walls were covered with gold leaf and the art of famous artists. For soldiers recently escaped from the horrors of the war in the Philippines and days in the air, the display of opulence overwhelmed us. When I peered into a lobby mirror and saw a tramp looking back, it made me uncomfortable and embarrassed.

"In the sanctuary of the hotel room I threw off my uniform, showered and shaved. Freshened and snug in a bathrobe supplied by the hotel, I pulled back the wooden shutters. A bottle of Champagne sat in a bucket of ice. I lit a cigarette and poured a glass of the sparkles then sank into a leather chair and looked out across the city skyline to the docks in the distance. I must admit, for a few moments the war slipped my mind as I experienced the life of the rich and famous. Then I gave thought to the mission. I had six men to protect the President of the United States? It would be impossible.

"As arranged, I met with Colonel Peron for dinner in the hotel restaurant. John Wayne and

Mandy joined us. The President sent his apologies. He wanted to retire early. Mandy had changed into a light blue satin evening gown that slid over her trim figure like a second skin. Dark hair framed an oval face. Her milky complexion only needed and a touch of make-up to highlight her fine features. Mandy out of uniform was an attractive woman, pretty enough to raise the eyebrows of Wayne and Peron. They sat her between them and fought each other to dominate the conversation. I sat at the end of the table. From time to time Mandy glanced my way and offered a smile and I must admit it raised my blood pressure a little.

"Then the restaurant lights dimmed. Applause broke out. I looked towards the entrance and then she appeared. Her blonde hair swept back into a chignon that nestled into the nape of her neck. A face so perfect it might have been chiseled from alabaster by the most skillful of craftsman. Her figure, slender, elegant, the poise of a dancer, and as she made her way to the centre of the ballroom floor she exuded a presence that was undeniable. She was the most beautiful, stunning young woman I had ever laid eyes upon. She stood before the microphone and waited for the applause to die. And then, waited some more. The silence was deafening. It was as if everyone in the restaurant had held their breath at the same time.

"Colonel Peron leaned across and whispered that we were about to listen to a reading from the most famous actress in all of Argentina, Miss Eva Duarte."

###

"Granddad," Sophie began. "This Eva Duarte. Is this the Eva that became Eva Peron?"

"The one and only," said Andrew.

"I watched a documentary on the Perons not so long ago," David said, "I'm certain that Eva and Juan Peron did not meet until near the end of the war."

"And now you know that wasn't true. The story behind the story; isn't that what journalism is all about?"

"I have an editor to convince and he pays my wages," David answered. Hesitant, uncertain as to what to believe anymore, but intrigued all the same.

"And what about Mandy?" Sophie asked.

"All in good time," Andrew said.

###

"Eva spoke in Spanish. I listened but did not understand. When the performance ended the rapturous applause continued long after Eva had gone.

"Peron filled our glasses with champagne: the real McCoy, I checked the label and it came from France. We toasted to her beauty and talent. The hotel manager approached our table. Apparently Eva Duarte had requested to join us. She wanted to meet the famous American actor John Wayne.

"We all stood when the manager brought her to our table.

73

"'Good evening Ma'am,' Wayne drawled.

"He was a big man and when he stood he was a commanding presence. Not about to be left wanting when it came to chivalry, Peron showed he was the perfect gentleman and took her hand, bowing before kissing it. He sat her next to himself. Not to be outdone, Wayne moved Mandy aside and sat on Eva's other side.

"I considered it my lucky night. I was never going to out-muscle Wayne and Peron for Eva Duarte's attention but I sure as hell was happy to have Mandy all to myself."

"Did Grandma know any of this?" Sophie teased.

"Darling, what went on between your grandmother and me is my business."

Andrew returned to his story.

"Early next morning the President sent for me. I was finally to be told why I had travelled the length of the globe. Wayne and General Beazley sat at the small dining table and I sat in the empty chair. Wayne looked a little the worse for wear, as I must have done myself. Too much champagne and cognac had taken its toll but neither Wayne nor Peron had wished to leave as long as Eva continued to enjoy their attentiveness. This was a damsel being pursued by two determined knights. Mandy and I had also stayed longer than we should have. However, this morning unlike the rest of us, she looked fresh.

"'Major Johnston, you must be wondering why you're here?' the President began. 'Why I dragged you from more important duties, like planning the reinvasion of the Philippines with MacArthur.'

"'I'm a soldier, sir,' I replied. 'I do as I'm told.'

"'All the same, Major, you're a soldier not a nursemaid. We have spies in Washington, everywhere in fact. It was important the American people never learn of this mission. That's why you and your men came from Australia and the pilots flew from England. No one in our great nation except for Mr Wayne, the General, his staff and Mandy of course, knew of my final destination. Someone leaked to the media that I have the flu. Nothing official. The government can't lie to the people.'

"'Now the why. A meeting will take place later today. Mr Wayne will chair this meeting. Why Mr Wayne for such an illustrious task? Well, believe it or not his movies have made him one of the world's most trusted and known men. His attendance is a sign of goodwill. Others attending figure that if it all turns sour, the American people might not care if their President ever returns home, but Mr Wayne is a different matter. Some consider him a national treasure. He is insurance, if you like, against dirty tricks. No one trusts us Americans. Some attending the meeting have promised to kill Mr Wayne if we try anything silly.'

"I looked at Wayne and received a shrug and a smile.

"'When the meeting starts, Major, you will sit at Mr Wayne's side,' President Roosevelt told me. 'I am going to ask you to take notes of the discussions and later take photographs. You can write?'"

"'Yes sir, I can write,' I told him."

"'Good man,' he said. 'Whatever you see and whatever you hear comes under the secrecy act. When the meeting is finished you will give the documents and photographs to the general. It can never be discussed. Not ever. Is that clear?'"

"'Yes sir,' I answered. 'May I ask who will be at the meeting?'

"'No you may not. You will report to Room 414 on the fourth floor at 1pm. Don't be late.'"

"In the hallway outside room 414 Peron had men everywhere. I waited as a soldier checked my ID. Peron looked on but did not intervene. Security by the book. I liked Peron. A professional.

"Once I gained my security clearance I entered the room.

"The men seated round the table were in deep discussion, not with each other but with aides, seated behind them. A few looked my way and after assessing my importance as zero returned to their conversations. I sat next to John Wayne as instructed. On the table in front of me sat a camera and notepad.

"As I looked over the attendees, my first emotion was confusion, then incredulity, then wonderment. I turned to Wayne. He had been watching me, waiting for my reaction. The grin that flashed across his face at my stunned-mullet response told me I had not disappointed him.

"They were all there, the leaders.

"Tojo sat in silence. Stiff-backed. He had the aloofness of a Shogun and the absolute assurance that his army of samurai believed he was a god. Of course, he was no more a Shogun than I was and his army of fanatical followers only resembled samurai warriors in that they would gladly lay down their life for their leader.

"De Gaulle made the most noise. Mussolini, Germany's unreliable ally, matched him for bluster. It was accepted by western military intelligence that the Italian led an army that preferred love, not war.

Hitler was all charm and geniality; the quintessential psychopath. Already so much blood on his hands and oblivious to the fact he was a monster. He glanced my way on one occasion. He reminded me of an undertaker and I had the distinct feeling those empty eyes were sizing me up for a body bag. Churchill sucked on a cigar and FDR kept saying Goddam's to everything. It was a circus. Then there was Stalin, the hardest to read. He had a wildness about him that was almost feral; a cornered lion with a thorn in its paw. The word 'vicious' came to mind. Of all the leaders in the room the persona of Stalin was the most dangerous. Not a man I would ever turn my back on.

"I opened my pad and fiddled with pens. Wayne asked if I was ready. I held up a pen and nodded. He stood and banged the table with a small gavel. The meeting started.

"Churchill, Roosevelt, De Gaulle and Stalin were on one side of the table, and Hitler, Tojo and Mussolini on the other side. Translators stood behind their leaders. Hitler made the opening speech, his translator careful to interpret Hitler's words and give emphasis on syllables to match the rhythm of the German dictator's oration. For a moment I felt transposed to a Nazi rally in Germany and heard what the German people must have heard. I found it hard to concentrate on note-taking. I was still reeling from the enormousness of the occasion, but as Hitler spoke on the meeting's objectives that had brought these world leaders together, my mouth fell open in horror. I turned to Wayne. The rhetoric had not disturbed him. He must have known the discussion topic beforehand which could be the only reason he had not collapsed into a dumbfounded stupor as I had done.

"Hitler finished and the arguing began in earnest."

Andrew leaned back, his eyes closed and he stayed silent. Sophie looked in David's direction. David raised an eyebrow then dropped his head to one side and tried to peer under Andrew's closed lids. He looked back at Sophie and shrugged.

"Granddad, are you okay," Sophie asked as she rubbed his arm.

Andrew opened his eyes and smiled, then touched her hand. "I'm sorry. It was so long ago but just for a moment the image became so clear. I could smell Churchill's cigar. I'm tired. I must be hallucinating."

"We should go."

"No, please stay. I've kept this story bottled up for too long."

David settled back. However, Sophie could read the signs. He was struggling with the credibility of the story unfolding. If she was honest she wasn't certain what to believe. But she knew her grandfather. He had never lied to her in all the conversations they had had throughout her childhood. He had always treated her as an adult. A reason for her continued visits even through her teen years. With Granddad she was a grown-up.

"What was it they were discussing?" David asked, genuine curiosity in his tone.

"The war had reached an impasse," Andrew said. "Germany had failed to invade Britain and was struggling in Russia. Japan was taking more and more of Asia but its forces and resources were stretched. Everyone in the room knew that the wealth and industry of America would tip the scales. But how long that would take was anyone's guess. This was a world war. Men and women and children had been killed by the millions and no end was in sight. The meeting was to discuss a truce and the carving up of the world along the existing lines of occupation."

"Who called the meeting?" David asked.

"Hitler. He had achieved what he had set out to gain: oil fields and industrial might. Now he saw it as time to crown himself King of Europe. With Japan as an able ally he could negotiate from a position of strength."

"Roosevelt and Churchill wouldn't have agreed to that, would they?" Sophie asked.

"In the beginning I did have my reservations, I must admit. Remember, Britain was vulnerable and just holding out. If Germany had tried to invade it might have been successful. De Gaulle argued against the proposal from the beginning. But his position was weak so no one paid him much heed. I never really understood why he was there."

"And the Pacific?" David asked.

"This was tricky. The Japanese wanted New Zealand and Australia, for obvious reasons. Britain couldn't fight on so many fronts and the US was more interested in Southern America. They had already agreed that the Middle East and Africa would be carved up at a later date."

"Jesus," David said. "And you recorded all this?"

"Not recorded, I took notes. But yes, I jotted down the gist of what was said, and took photos. The camera, photos and my notes would be confiscated before we returned to the US. Roosevelt wanted me to develop the film in my room later in the evening. Even today all documents remain under the umbrella of the Official Secrets Act. If I ever opened my mouth I could lose my military pension."

"Then why tell us, Granddad?"

"I'm an old man. All the main players are dead."

David said, "And about the photographs? I can't believe these men allowed themselves to be photographed."

"Politicians were no different then, than they are today. Stroke their feathers and they will preen. Especially, this group. A football stadium would not have been big enough to hold their egos."

"That still doesn't explain why John Wayne was there to chair the meeting?" Sophie asked.

Andrew smiled.

"Hitler was a fan of American movies. He had his own private cinema and most nights would watch a movie - movies denied to German citizens, so I'm told. Typical dictator. I can't think of a single dictator in history who led by example. Anyway, he was a huge John Wayne fan and insisted Roosevelt include Wayne and have him host the meeting. In my opinion, if ever there was a sign the man was insane it was the moment he made that decision. There he was, slaughtering humans by the millions, and he turns out to be a closet adulating groupie. If Mickey Mouse had been for real he would have been there instead of Wayne. Hitler loved Mickey Mouse and, ironically, Jewish comedians. So anyway, that's how Wayne came to be there."

"And not Mickey Mouse," Sophie laughed.

"Like boxers, they eyed each other. A touch of gloves. Then the sniping began in earnest. Stalin remained a non-participant, watching, seemingly relaxed and uninterested, but those beady eyes missed nothing. Churchill and Roosevelt nodded like puppets in a fairground. Then I noticed that although they were nodding, the nods were not in agreement to comments made, just hollow gestures. Then Stalin leaned forward.

"'Enough,' he yelled and banged his fist on the table.

"I almost jumped out of my seat. The others stopped talking. All eyes were on Stalin as he rose. He jabbed his finger at Hitler and Mussolini. 'I refuse to listen to these sons of pigs any longer.'

"Stalin glared at Hitler, and for a moment I feared he was about to leap across the table and throttle the little Nazi shit. Hitler held Stalin's glare but the uncertainty was there and he blinked first. Then the sort of tirade Hitler was famous for spat forth. It was Stalin's turn to smile. I saw Roosevelt smirk and a quick flick of his eyes towards Churchill. Then everyone started screaming and yelling. Wayne let it continue for a few minutes then banged his gavel and got to his feet. His size demanded attention and, of course, he was an actor. He gave his best mean look; the one that had caused countless Hollywood baddies to tremble.

"The astonished leaders fell silent. Their interpreters and body guards were unsure how to react so did nothing. Stalin sat first and then Wayne sank back in his chair. The tension eased. He had established himself as a chairman who would tolerate no nonsense. If only movie cameras had been rolling, it was his finest performance."

"From that moment FDR and Churchill knew they would win the war. The alliance between Britain, Russia and the US was forged," Andrew said.

"How so?" Sophie asked. "If they were about to agree to carve up the world a few minutes before, what changed that they could be certain they would win the war?"

"Because neither Roosevelt nor Churchill had ever considered the truce a serious option. For them their reason for attending the meeting was Stalin. Before the war Stalin had signed a treaty with Hitler. Roosevelt and Churchill were unsure that with the German army surrounding Moscow and over-running Stalingrad, that Stalin might grasp at the offer of a truce to save his ass. His outburst said all they needed to hear. Stalin hated Hitler and Russia would fight Germany to the bitter end. Hitler could never win fighting on so many fronts."

"So you're saying that you consider this meeting a turning point in the Second World War?" David asked.

"Yes. Prior to the Argentina meeting the war had gone the way of the axis powers. After Argentina the German advance lost momentum and the Japanese faltered. Like good boxers, the allied leaders had looked their opponents in the eye and seen weakness and smelt victory."

"And that was that," Sophie said. "Did you go back to Australia?"

"It wasn't over, Sophie. Not by a long shot. Later that day John Wayne went missing."

"The smoke clouds puffing from Roosevelt's cigar reminded me of a steam locomotive. Something was up. Mandy stood behind him, her brow furrowed. The President's spare hand slapped on the arm of his chair. He did not ask me to sit.

"'Major Johnston,' he said. 'Mr Wayne has gone missing. I need you to find him asap. The plane leaves in three hours. I can't go home and leave him behind, can I?'

"'No, Mr President, you cannot,' I replied.

"As I stood there I flicked through a few scenarios in my head but had to concede that where Wayne might have run off to was beyond me. He had never been to Argentina before. He

84

didn't know anyone. I would need to speak to Juan Peron.

"'I'll go find him sir,'" I told the President.

"'Mandy, go with him. Two sets of eyes, and all that.'

"For the President's benefit I accepted the offer of Mandy's help with the dignity the offer deserved. A few hours with Mandy was a pleasure I looked forward to. I could not take any of my men from his protection detail. Losing John Wayne would be bad enough, but losing the President unthinkable.

"We met up with Colonel Peron in the foyer. I explained what had taken place.

"'This is very serious. Mr Wayne should not wander the streets of Buenos Aries unprotected,' Peron said.

"'I can only think he's gone to meet with Miss Duarte; he knows no one else,' I said.

"Peron nodded. 'Eva will be at the Radio theatre. She performs every afternoon around this time and the whole country tunes in. This she would never miss.'

"Peron bundled us into his military vehicle and instructed the driver where to go.

"'John Wayne. He is a ladies' man?' Peron asked me.

"'He is a film star, Colonel. I think ladies come with the territory.'

"'He is married isn't he?' Mandy asked.

"Peron smiled at me and neither of us deigned to answer her. What could we say? Not what we were thinking. That Eva Duarte was a very beautiful woman and would turn the head of the strongest of men. Married or not.

"Peron worried that Wayne might have come to harm. The city was abuzz with Japanese and German agents. Neither lot would hesitate to kill someone of Wayne's stature in a gesture to lower American morale. However, I dismissed the idea. Hitler had nothing to gain by embarrassing the President of the United States. At least, not before he had received an answer to his proposal. There was little doubt the American public would not understand Roosevelt's reasons for attending the meeting. To be honest, it was a question I asked myself. To have Hitler and Hirohito that close and not put a bullet in their skulls, it would have been difficult to explain away.

"Peron left Mandy and me in the car when we reached the radio station. He returned after a few minutes.

"'Neither your Mr Wayne nor Eva Duarte are at the station. I think we can conclude that wherever they might be, they are together.'

"'Does Eva have an apartment?' I asked.

"'They would not go there. Miss Duarte is a woman of high standing. She would not take a man to her apartment. Even a man such as Mr Wayne.'"

"'Where then?'"

"'In Buenos Aries if a man and a woman want to be alone they might walk in the park. Or, along the water's edge. Many people use the park. They would be recognised so I think the foreshore. There is plenty of it. They could find some private space easy enough.'

"Peron gave an instruction to his driver and we found ourselves travelling through the shanty town that separated the central city from the docks. We drove along the front of the port until we could see the sandy coastline that stretched until it disappeared into a cloudy haze. After ten minutes we pulled up beside a café. Wayne and Eva were standing beside the water's edge. We decided not to interrupt the liaison. There was time to spare. Peron ordered coffees and we sat and watched."

"Were they cuddling?" Sophie asked.

"No, of course not," Andrew said pretending to scold Sophie. "By today's standards it was all perfectly innocent but back then, a man and a woman alone, well… it just wasn't done. Tongues would wag. Was Wayne besotted with Eva? I don't know. That they enjoyed each other's company there was no doubt. If there had not been a war maybe he might have returned to Argentina. The look she gave him when they parted left me in no doubt he would be welcome. But there was a war, and by the time it was over Juan and Eva had married.

"So Wayne and Eva never saw each other again?"

"Not that I'm aware of. But I'm certain Wayne never forgot her. In 1953 he made a movie called *Honcho*. This was a year after Eva died, the first film he made after her death. In a scene near the end his character is looking across a landscape at the setting sun. He says 'the blood red sky is the same in Buenos Aries where sadly a light that shone so brightly for me has dimmed'. I believe this was Wayne's tribute to Eva. It's how Wayne would have done it. Actor to actor."

Andrew sat back in his seat.

"And there you have it. A few days in Argentina that changed history in so many ways."

"Interesting story, Mr Johnston," David said.

"Aha," Andrew said, a mischievous sparkle in his eye. "This is where a true journalist grasps the few threads of information and runs with it. Follows their gut instinct."

"My instincts tell me it would be impossible to research," David said. "Sophie and I would have nowhere to begin. You are the only living person who attended this meeting and you can't give us anything to back up your story. There is no trail. Even the John Wayne quote in the movie is meaningless unless the rest of the story can be corroborated."

"I'm afraid I have to agree with David, Granddad," Sophie added. "With the whole event

88

archived to the American national security bin and most of the players now dead, all roads are closed."

"And you two call yourselves journalists. I've given you one of the great war stories of the twentieth century. Your eyes should be filled with fire."

"I'm sorry, Mr Johnston," David said. "We have to work with facts. It's a great story, but without evidence that the meeting took place, it is only fiction. Do you have a stamped passport? A copy of your orders from McArthur?"

"Nothing like that, David. In those days no one had passports and orders for a secret mission were not written down. At least, not written down and handed out like a newsletter."

David stood up. "I'm sorry, but for us to rewrite history, and this is rewriting history, we need supporting documents to show it took place. Great yarn Mr Johnston, I'll give you that and I enjoyed listening to it, but it is just a yarn, no more." He looked at his watch. "Come on Sophie we need to get down to the RSA. We can still catch a few of the old soldiers."

Sophie stayed sitting and stroked her grandfather's arm.

"Let's put it off until tomorrow night. Granddad's tired. I want to stay with him awhile. Get him to eat some dinner."

David, uncomfortable, eyed Andrew then flicked back to Sophie.

"No go, Sophie. It needs to be tonight. If I go it alone, well, you know it will be my project. The editor won't be happy."

"I'll take my chances," Sophie said.

David clenched his teeth.

"Right then. Your decision, but I'm off and I won't be back. You'll need to find your own way back to your car."

When Sophie heard the door close and was certain David had left, she turned her attention back to her grandfather.

With a worried look on his face, Andrew said, "You can spend the night here. I hope I haven't got you into trouble."

Sophie shrugged, then smiled, "Don't worry Granddad, I'm a big girl. You always said a good journalist needs instincts," Sophie began. "My instincts tell me you have evidence of the meeting in Buenos Aries."

Andrew smiled.

"Of course I do. In the scrapbook is a copy of the photos and notes I made before handing them over. I would have shown you earlier, but your friend never asked. He just told me I didn't have anything. "

Sophie hugged her grandfather.

"I'll make us some dinner then you can show me the secret stash."

The end

The Best of Times

I call myself a writer. Not really true. Writers write. I, however, spend my time searching for inspiration to prove my literary genius – and have never managed to write a single word. My disheartened father has labelled me bone idle. My ever-tolerant mother, God bless her, fought to restore my place in dear Father's heart and managed to win sufficient minor battles to at least ensure I was never rendered penniless. I always have enough money to pursue nothingness to my heart's content.

Each afternoon I would walk across the sands of Mission Bay recovering from the night before and preparing for the night to come. One particular day, as I stood at the water's edge letting small waves nuzzle my ankles, I caught sight of the mountain peak on Rangitoto Island silhouetted against a blood-red sky. It looked like an exploding volcano. I was held in awe for some minutes by nature's violent image. She had been affected by it too. Evelyn. It was the first time I'd ever seen her.

Jeans rolled up, she stood ankle-deep in the water some yards away. When she bent to allow an incoming ripple to wash over her fingers her elegance of movement reminded me of a ballet dancer.

"Imposing or majestic?" I called, moving a little closer.

"I prefer *celestial*. It's more comforting."

"Interesting answer and I'd say it comes from a pure heart, easy to love and easily wounded. You spend much of your time between tears and laughter but you are never maudlin. You never...*dwell*."

"A student of astrology, I see."

"Not at all. I read the lines in a book and thought I'd use them to make myself sound clever." I smiled. "Did it work?"

Evelyn's spontaneous tinkle of laughter was accompanied by a playful touch of my arm. And I was under her spell.

"I'm Jack."

"I'm Evelyn."

For the next two months Evelyn and I wined, dined and laughed. But there was no sex. We never so much as made out. I stood forlorn under the pedestal I had placed her on and lusted for even just the smell of her. And every Sunday we joined others at her father's house for poetry readings. If asked, I would have said I found poetry about as desirable as an abscessing tooth, thus my dislike of William Lambert's poetry went without saying. But

Evelyn did like it, and Lambert was her father so I tolerated his work. In the beginning I did try to gain an understanding of his poetic prowess but I couldn't see what his fans saw and gave up trying.

The chosen ten gathered on the back deck of Lambert's home and listened to his recitations. Eight adoring students from Lambert's literature class soaked up the words spouting forth from the man they considered a master wordsmith. Evelyn listened and I sat in patient anticipation of the conclusion. The late afternoon breeze would ruffle Evelyn's hair, teasing her mesh of red tresses into gentle caresses about her shoulders. I marveled at how her hair could turn to shimmering gold as the sun set.

After the reading, and with darkness falling, lamps would be lit. We drank wine and listened as Lambert pontificated on the meaning and relevance of his words. In the discussions that followed, Lambert always rubbished my interpretations, especially when I'd said in an unguarded moment that his poetry reminded me of the verses in greeting cards. The evenings always descended into drunken rambling. And I would set about emptying his wine bottles with all the enthusiasm I was incapable of mustering for his blank verse. Or was it dead crap? As this particular evening deteriorated, at some stage Lambert stood, leaned over hands that supported him on the table, and fixed his sights on me.

"*You* should not be seated at this table. You're not worthy to be in the presence of anything even remotely resembling intellectual discussion."

A sway, and he slumped back into his seat.

No particular riposte coming to mind, I said nothing. I'd long accepted the role of court jester as it allowed me to linger in the company of the lovely Evelyn. It didn't bother me that she never rose to my defence. I understood her reasons. Evelyn detested conflict in any form. For me, I'd learned just to sip my wine in silence. Thankfully, once Lambert had spoken his mind I became pretty much non-existent for the rest of that evening. These evenings were all about Lambert and he brooked no upstaging.

To signal the evening's end Lambert would select a student and stagger off to his bedroom. At this juncture the others would depart, whether from the disappointment of not being the night's sacrificial lamb, or the fear that Lambert might decide to return and choose somebody else, I never really determined.

But patience does reap rewards.

After weeks invested in suffering Lambert's ridicule, payback arrived. His daughter took me to her bed.

How Lambert knew the exact moment I began sleeping with his daughter I will never know. But after that night, whenever his piercing blue eyes fixed upon mine, I would shift in my seat and marvel at how insignificant a man could be made to feel.

One night on my way to the bathroom, Lambert intercepted me in the hallway and steered me into his study. The stink of whisky on him darn near knocked me out. He sat balanced on the edge of his desk, fists clenched like a boxer readying to throw a knockout punch. I edged away so that at least a corner of the desk intervened between him and a very tense body. But then his shoulders slumped. Fists flattened and rubbed down his trouser legs as if wiping away sweat.

From me a slow release of breath.

Lambert's bloodshot eyes rose.

"A word of warning. Whatever you do, do not offer Evelyn marriage or a life together. If you truly love her, as you seem to believe, make a grand gesture and back out now."

Without another word he staggered from the room. I wanted to dismiss the incident as the reaction of an over-protective father. But a storm cloud settled over my soul, and my inner voice screamed at me that Lambert had sent me a message – run for my life.

When I thought through the times Evelyn and I lay in bed and talked, it had always been about *my* life, *my* aspirations. Whenever I questioned Evelyn's past, she told me only of her dreams for the future. When we made love her motivation appeared to be more a willingness to please than a search for mutual satisfaction. She never experienced orgasms. It was not a topic she would discuss and so I continued to fulfill my own needs convincing myself that Evelyn was finding equal fulfillment.

During one of these frenzied bouts of passion, I forced myself up onto my arms to gain increased thrust. I looked directly into her eyes. Moonlight through the curtains illuminated her face. Her eyes were not searching for mine. They remained fixed on a spot on the ceiling, face devoid of expression. The sounds of her fake orgasm suddenly rang hollow in my ears.

Hours later when I woke, Evelyn had gone.

I phoned a friend. She worked in a women's refuge centre. Over a few drinks one night she had horrified me with stories of the abuse suffered by women seeking shelter. She said she had seen it all, and after years of listening and advising the battered and broken of spirit she considered herself a cross between a psychiatrist and a psychologist, even though she held no formal qualification.

"From what you're telling me she bears the classic symptoms of sexual abuse; personality shift, reluctance to commit. What has she told you of her childhood?"

"Nothing much," I said. "Whenever the topic comes up she changes the subject."

"I could meet with her if she wants. Ask a few questions but really, this is a specialist area. She should be talking with a doctor. Have you suggested this to her?"

"Let me think about it. I'll get back to you."

Lambert paled. He leaned forward, eyes clamped onto mine like the guidance system of a Trident Missile.

"You accuse me of this heinous crime? Against my own *daughter*? "

The vehemence of Lambert's protestation shot flashes through my brain. My brow furrowed, suddenly doubtful. What if I was wrong? Lambert rose from his chair. My senses went on the alert. Although I was the bigger man, I knew that passion could increase a man's strength. And that Lambert was incensed there could be no doubt: his knuckles made unnerving crunching sounds as they ground into the oak desktop.

The finger he suddenly pointed into my face caused me to recoil.

He said, "There you stand. My daughter's guardian, is it? The rock for her to tether her hopes on? You. The laird to whom we peasants must pay homage and be ever so grateful that you are the sentinel, our protection from the gates of hell. And why is that? Why do you think you have a right to do this? I'll tell you. Because you have this certainty, assuredness that the motives for your actions are noble, but they are not. You are an egotistical nobody jumping to conclusions. A caped crusader with the cape pulled over your head. You want to be the hero that saves my Evelyn? Hah. You *will* not because you *can* not." The finger lowered. "Now, where is she? What have you done with her?"

"She's in a safe place. I left her with a friend at the women's refuge. They are talking. She will unlock the door to the reason for Evelyn's suffering and heal her. It's over, Lambert. You're about to be found out."

"You fool. You self-obsessed insignificant piece of vermin. Yes, she was abused when she was young. But it was not in any way as you think." Lambert reached into his desk drawer and pulled out a picture frame and let it fall onto the desktop. "See that. A photo of my family. A very happy family."

Lambert slumped into his chair.

"The woman is Evelyn's mother, Rachel. As you can see she was a woman of great beauty and I loved and adored her. Despite my failings she chose to be part of my life and that decision gave me the confidence to pour my soul onto paper and make my inner feelings public. I reasoned that if I could conquer Rachel then conquering the world of literature seemed a simple task. The girl is Evelyn - taken a few days after her sixteenth birthday. It was taken in the highlands of New Guinea. Rachel wanted to help the less fortunate. Do missionary work. She accepted a six-month teaching post in a remote village. It was to be a

98

great adventure and I agreed she could take Evelyn."

An unsteady hand lifted the whisky decanter at his elbow. Brown liquid slopped into a glass. One gulp and half vanished down his throat. A fit of coughing followed, during which his efforts at placing the tumbler down again only succeeded in splashing amber liquid down his shirt front. His eyes fixed on me once more. Not hostile now. More as if he was at the end of a very long road.

"It was midday. The children had been sent out to eat their lunch and play. When Evelyn rang the bell, the children didn't come. She and Rachel went looking for them. It was Rachel who spotted legs protruding from under the bushes that bordered the playground. Twenty children. Lying side by side. The tops of their skulls cracked open. Their brains scooped out.

"A few metres away the tribesmen sat watching them, the grey of human offal dribbling from the black of their chins." Lambert's eyes fell to the photograph. His voice lost all expression. "It took a week before the authorities arrived. They were far too late. Rachel and Evelyn had been raped daily and with each defilement, a piece of their soul was wrenched from their chests. The women the authorities returned to me were not my wife and daughter."

The whisky bottle went to Lambert's lips. A deep swig then he thudded it onto the desk and pushed it towards me. I stared at it. Lambert's head buried into his hands. I waited. Not moving. Hardly daring to breathe.

"A year after she came home I found Rachel in the garage. She had tied tea towels together, enough to make a hangman's rope. I had lost my muse, my reason to exist, but I still had Evelyn. My beautiful, beautiful, baby." Bloodshot eyes fixed on mine. "And now, you have taken her from me. Opening the door to the past will destroy her. I warned you. Let it be on your head."

He thumped his fist on the table and tried to rise. But the alcohol had begun its work. He slid from his seat and collapsed onto the floor.

When I made it back to Jenny's, I found her in the sitting room. Evelyn sat on the floor, rocking back and forth. Jenny looked at me and shook her head. I backed away. Jenny followed, closing the door behind her.

"Her mind has retreated into another world. I can't get through to her."

"Jesus. How long will it last?"

"I don't know. I've called a doctor. He's on his way."

I told Jenny what I had heard from Lambert. She frowned.

"Best you wait in the kitchen."

Half an hour passed, and I made a coffee.

An hour, and a rummage around found me paper and a pen.

And words began to come.

###

A month passed, or maybe two, but one Sunday I found myself standing outside Lambert's house with no clear reason in my head as to why. Evelyn was in a retreat. I had been to visit every week. Each time I held her hand for the hour visit and never once in the hour did she acknowledge me. And now I had come to Lambert's.

I heard voices.

The pathway to the back of the house led me past weed-filled flower patches and unkempt shrubbery. On the deck they were two people: Lambert and a young woman – a student.

He watched as I climbed the three steps.

"What brings *you* here? To listen to my poetry? I think not." A sharp exhalation via flared nostrils. "Guilt? Let me guess. You seek redemption, exoneration? Well, fuck you."

Lambert's eyes widened as I stepped forward and drew up a chair. It had been a mistake to come and Lambert was right. I needed to be purged of culpability for Evelyn's cataleptic condition. Lambert planted elbows on table. Mouth curled into a snarl.

"I *warned* you. I *told* you."

His shaky hand tried to pour wine into a glass. The glass clattered onto its side and liquid slopped onto the timber. Lambert may have been drunk but those piercing eyes still managed to convey such an intensity of disdain that my last vestiges of resolve were reduced to shreds. I wanted to leave but I had turned to lead.

"Fuck you. My daughter is dead to me. You may as well have plunged a knife into her heart."

Unsteady hands on the table edge for support, Lambert stood and reached for the arm of his student. Her eyes looked like those of a frightened lamb with a butcher's knife at its throat. For an instant they flashed out what could have been a plea for help. But immature adulation for the aged poet must have trumped all other considerations. Her gaze dropped away and her arms made to assist the old guy. I raised my glass in salute to yet another female preparing to crash on the human wasteland that was Lambert.

They made a slow exit into the house.

I sat for a long time drinking his wine.

In the dark.

The end

The Chest

Air inside the bus clung with the feel and smell of a damp blanket. Darby rubbed the frosting off the window with the sleeve of his jacket then pushed his freckled face against the glass. An involuntary jerk away as a wave of water from an oncoming car arced at him like a slap in the face.

Money.

That screaming match between mum and dad in the kitchen had all been about money. Want of money. Waste of money. Never enough money. A hand stole into his jean pocket to ensure it was still there: the ten-dollar note he'd got from Grandpa for his birthday. It was enough for two return tickets should Grandpa not be at home in Sheltered Cove. A quick glance at his little sister seated alongside him. With relief he saw May was absorbed in one of her whispered conversations into the ear of Mr Bunny. His bottom lip began to tremble. A knuckle-wipe of his eyes and then his attention returned to looking through the window.

He did not want May to see he was frightened. Unsure he had made the right decision.

Darby was pretty certain he had thought of everything. When Mum and Dad planned a trip they always made a list. He had made a list of sorts. Empty his and May's cash tins, walk to the bus station, buy two bus tickets and find Grandpa's house. He guessed that was all there was to it. His mum would have said he could do it. She would have said you're a big boy now. You can do anything you want to do. But this had always confused him. Whenever he tried to do whatever he wanted, Mum growled at him. Nothing made sense when dealing with grown-ups.

He stole another look at little May. She had fallen asleep. He knew she thought he was big. But then, everything is big when you're five. He hated that she followed him everywhere, especially when his friends came to play. But his mother insisted he had to put up with it and look out for May. And he did. It helped that Mum gave him little rewards. Like cake and extra money for the movies.

Anyway, May didn't make a lot of noise. Just sat quietly and watched mostly. Sometimes she asked questions he had no answers for. So he invented answers. She trusted him and never appeared to doubt him.

But today the lie he told May was quite different.

To convince her to join him on his adventure, he had said their mother and father said it was okay. That she would not get into trouble. Now, after the long bus ride on this grey and heavy day, he wasn't so confident he had made a good decision.

To come all this way. What if Grandpa wasn't home?

If Grandpa had a phone he could have called first to make sure. But Grandpa refused to have a phone in the huge old house that he always seemed to be renovating in the mass of native bush back from the beach.

The bus slowed.

Darby nudged his sister.

"We're here, May."

May yawned. She glanced around like a startled deer, then relaxed. She rubbed her eyes and held Mr Bunny close to her chest and rocked back and forth until the bus came to a halt. Darby watched her ready to offer comfort should she become distressed.

May's earnest little face rose to view him.

"I don't know if I'm going to like it here, Darby."

"Don't be like that, May. We've been to Grandpa's plenty of times. Mr Bunny will have lots of bunny friends here. Not like in the city. You're a big girl now, remember?"

"No I'm not. I'm only five. I'm not six."

Darby shook his head. He had to be careful. An argument would set her crying, and that he didn't need right now. He helped her down the two steps.

When the bus drove away Darby took May's hand and led her across the road. It had stopped raining. May stomped in a puddle and splashed water everywhere. Giggling, she went to jump into a larger one but Darby pulled on her arm.

"We don't have time. Come on." May's bottom lip dropped. "I'll buy you an ice-cream later if you're good."

This had the desired effect. She beamed and slipped her hand from Darby's and skipped ahead down Main Street.

The village of Sheltered Cove was as Darby remembered: six shops and the hotel. The shops were on one side of the street and the hotel directly opposite. Darby remembered that when it got dark, the hotel got noisy. The grown-ups would sit in the window drinking beer. On the last holiday he had sat in the take-away drinking a milkshake and waiting for an order of fish and chips. His father and his grandfather had watched over him through the hotel window.

Today was only the second time he had been back since Grandma went away. He missed Grandma. Why she had left Grandpa his parents would never tell him. "Grown-ups' business," he was told. It was always grown-ups' business, and lately, when they argued and he asked what was wrong, it was more grown-ups' business. Only this time he found out for himself. He hadn't gone to his room. He had stayed in the hallway and listened.

And money was the reason he had come to the Cove.

He made a mistake letting May's hand go. She and Mr Bunny were engrossed in another conversation and now lagging behind. Darby waited for her to catch up. His sister hated long walks and he didn't want to carry her. He'd have to slow down. He took May's hand again and led her along the dirt track that ran down behind the hot pools and along the beachfront. The camping ground was full. He would ask Grandpa to bring them down to play on the trampoline later.

"Look. You can see Grandpa's house."

May looked up. Her face brightened at the sight of the 1930s' mustard-coloured bungalow set back amongst the bush. She ran ahead and across the unmown lawn. Weeds had overrun the garden and entwined themselves round Grandma's spiky rose stems. May jumped onto the wood decking and stopped at the front door.

Darby knocked twice and waited. He lifted himself onto tip-toes and peered as best he could through the crinkly red glass panel for any sign of life. He knocked again but heard only an empty echo from inside. He tried the handle. The door opened. May pushed past him and rushed inside.

"Grandpa. Grandpa. Where are you?"

Darby followed her. Now that Grandpa lived alone, coming to visit was not the same. When

Grandma was here there was always the smell of baking. That's how he remembered her always in the kitchen baking goodies.

He remembered how sad everyone had been when she went. His parents had told him not to mention Grandma in front of Grandpa. Of course, they forgot to tell May and she asked Grandpa where Grandma had gone. Luckily Darby had been on his guard so before his parents could admonish her he had taken her from the room. They'd played Ludo for the rest of that afternoon.

The whine of a drill met Darby's ears.

"He's in the kitchen, May".

May's little legs sped her down the hall and around the corner past the stand with coats hanging on it and an assortment of umbrellas. A squeal of delight came out of her.

"Grandpa. It's me and Darby."

Darby fell in behind May at the kitchen door. There was a wide-eyed Grandpa in his old leather carpenter's apron. A chewed-end pencil sat tucked behind his ear.

"Goodness me. What are you two doing here?"

To Darby Grandpa sounded more alarmed than pleased, though he was managing to raise half a smile.

"Mummy doesn't know we've come," May blurted out.

Grandpa's eyes became saucer-shaped. The smile disappeared.

"Darby, what's this all about, in heaven's name?"

Darby felt his courage deserting him. He grabbed May's hand.

"Please don't be mad, Grandpa. Mum and Dad were fighting. We didn't know where else to go," Darby said.

Grandpa's eyes switched from Darby to May and back. A hand rose to scratch the bald patch on top of his head. "Okay, no harm done. This is the right place to come. But your parents will be worried. How did you get here?"

"On the bus," Darby said. "I've been on a bus before. I know how to buy tickets."

"Yes, of course you do." Grandpa bent over, "You see kids, mums and dads fight all the time. They don't mean anything. Look, I'll have to go into the town and phone them. To let them know you're safe."

Grandpa turned and swung open the fridge door. He withdrew two cans of cola and put them on the table.

"Have a drink, kids. Stay here and I'll try not to be too long."

May tugged on the nail pouch of grandpa's apron.

"Mummy will be mad at us, won't she, Grandpa?"

"I'm sure she won't. Don't worry, darling. All will be well. But we don't want Mummy to worry, do we? Do you want me to bring back some fish and chips for your lunch?"

"That would be great, Grandpa," Darby said. He rubbed his stomach. It had been a long time since breakfast. Grandpa unbuckled his apron and tossed it on the table.

"Very well, I'm going now. May, be a good girl and do what Darby says. Okay?"

"I will."

Darby waited until he heard the front door close.

"Right, Come on May. We need to get into the attic and find the map."

"Grandpa said to stay here."

"He said you have to do what I tell you too. So, let's go find the map. Come on."

Halfway down the hallway Darby reached up and pulled on the cord that brought down the folding steps that gave access to the roof cavity. He was remembering how their grandfather had said to them many times that they weren't to play in the attic. But that was when Darby was much younger. It surely wouldn't count now that he was older and bigger.

May tugged at his arm.

"Grandpa won't growl at us, will he?"

"Course he won't. Look, as soon as we finish I'll buy you an ice-cream."

The smile returned.

The old trunk was covered in dust but in the same spot that Darby remembered. May stood behind him. He knew she hated the attic. Jenny, her friend at school, had told her ghosts lived in attics and dead people were always found in old trunks. Darby slid back the bolt and lifted the lid wide. A creak and a cloud of dust met his efforts. A clink as a chain at one side tightened and took the weight of the lid. Darby reached into the interior and pulled out a document. He unrolled it on the floor. May moved closer.

"There it is the cross like I remembered it. Wow. Look, here is the house. That's the beach down there, and that's the big tree out the back. We need to walk fifty paces into the bush. It's there. See the X? That's where the treasure is. Come on. We have to hurry."

May shook her head and tightened her grip on Mr Bunny. Darby stood and pointed to the stairs.

"Look, May. If we find the treasure then Mum and Dad won't fight anymore. They'll have enough money to pay the bills. Okay? You want to help Mum and Dad don't you?"

May nodded.

"Come on. I'll get a spade from Grandpa's shed. We can dig up the treasure before he gets back."

"I'm too little to dig holes."

Digging was boring and Darby had not found any treasure. Only old bones and other rubbish and the bracelet he and May had bought Grandma for her birthday. He remembered it because it had

111

'From D and M' engraved on it. She must have dropped it gardening. He suspected all he'd found was the bone hiding place for Grandpa's neighbour's dog.

May sat on a tree stump. She was talking to Mr Bunny when she heard the scrunch of twigs behind her. She jumped off the stump and ran to stand beside Darby.

"Someone's coming."

Darby stopped his digging as Grandpa's figure emerged through the bushes. The face that confronted Darby alarmed him. Grandpa's tanned skin looked to have gone tight and quite yellow.

"What are you doing?"

"Digging a hole, Grandpa," May said. "Darby is looking for the treasure. Is Mummy coming?"

"Not yet. She wasn't home. I will phone again later. You're looking for treasure Darby?"

"Yes, Grandpa. But all I found was old dog bones and stuff and Grandma's bracelet, look." He held it up.

Grandpa's narrowed eyes fixed on the disturbed soil at Darby's feet.

"Dog bones? Oh yes. Of course. But why on earth would you think there's treasure buried here?"

Darby looked at the ground and pushed at a sod of earth with the toe of his shoe.

"I found the treasure map in the trunk in the attic."

Grandpa's eyebrows concentrated above the bridge of his nose.

"Darby. How many times have I told you to stay out of the attic?"

"I'm sorry, but I had to. The reason Mum and Dad have been fighting is because of money. We saw a movie last week. The children were sent to an orphanage. Me and May...."

Darby looked at May. Her bottom lip was trembling. She turned imploring eyes up to her grandfather.

"Pleeease Grandpa. I don't want to be an orphan."

Grandpa took a step towards Darby. He reached for the spade and jammed it into the ground in front of him and leaned on it. Darby couldn't help but notice the whites of the knuckles on the strong hands that gripped the handle. Grandpa stayed like that for a long moment surveying his grandchildren. With a deep intake of breath he straightened.

"Don't worry, darling. I promise you won't be an orphan."

"Hi Dad. Have you seen Darby and May? Are they here?"

"No June. Why would they be? You stopped them coming here remember."

June ignored the comment.

"They've run away. John and I have been fighting a lot lately. The kids must have got frightened and gone off somewhere."

Grandpa gave his daughter a steady look.

"Gone off? Well, well. Got that from your mother, I suppose. Any handsome face and she'd be off. Then back when they'd had enough of her. Anyway, this old place is too far out for the kids. How would they even know how to get here?"

"I suppose you're right. I wish you'd get a phone in. Okay, I've got to get back home. If they turn up, please phone me."

"Of course I will. Don't worry, I'm sure they're safe."

Grandpa watched the back of his daughter disappear, then closed the door. He walked down the hallway into the kitchen and took down the whisky bottle from the cupboard over the fridge. He half-filled a glass then made his way back to the hall and pulled on the cord for the stairs up to the attic.

He knelt before the wooden chest and opened it.

He took out the map. Looked at the X.

The chewed-up pencil came from behind Grandpa's ear.

It descended onto the map.

Two small crosses appeared beside the original one.

The end

The Wooden Sword

The old man stayed in the shadows of the doorway. His eyes fixed on the store opposite searching for the unusual. Seeking any sign of movement. An hour had passed and he could wait no longer.

As he crossed the street rain ricocheted off his hat and spattered across the shoulders of his black cashmere overcoat. Rivulets dribbled down the sleeves and transformed into bulging droplets along the seam of the upturned cuff before cascading down onto his Italian patent leather shoes. An ivory-handled cane grasped tightly in his right hand prevented the old man's giant frame from falling forward and crashing onto the cobblestoned pavement. Shoulders hunched, it took him enormous effort to move his creaking physique, each step bringing a quickness of breath and a grunt of pain.

He stopped in front of the Old Curio Shop.

Flickering fingers of light splashed out from lamps atop undusted tables glimmering across the window's grimy glass pane. The result enough of a mirror to reflect the old man's lined, ashen visage; an impassive face, unemotional, as if chiseled from granite and weathered by the forces of nature for a century or more. The wooden object stood in the rustic earthen ewer hidden amongst used umbrellas and walking sticks. The corners of his thin lips turned upwards offering the merest hint of a smile.

His prize was there to collect.

A bell dangling from a piece of string jingled as he pushed the door open and rang again as he closed it. A musty atmosphere emanating from the old and ancient hung in the enclosed environment like smog. It clogged his sinuses and brought on a coughing fit, causing him to halt his progress and catch his breath. He produced a handkerchief and wiped spittle from his lips. The pathway between the rows of borer-ridden cabinets displaying chipped china plates and ornaments was a strip of worn carpet. When he made it to the counter, he used it to prop himself up and pushed the buzzer.

The shopkeeper appeared through the plastic dangling strips; fat, sweaty, underarms that needed deodorant and a mouth that reeked halitosis. He eyed his customer and the initial hostile glare of annoyance was now replaced by an insincere smile at an anticipated sale.

"The umbrella stand in the window. The wood cane. I want to buy it."

The old man's voice was deep and gravelly, like the sound of pebbles and sand churning in a concrete mixer. It carried an edge, an authority.

"It's not for sale."

"No, of course it isn't," the old man agreed. "The light in the window is a light for me."

The fat shop-keeper stiffened at the old man's words then nodded. He rubbed a grubby hand across the t-shirt stretched over his beer belly and spotted with a trail of tomato sauce and cooking oil stains.

"There is a payment."

"One hundred dollars," the old man said. He took two fifty-dollar notes from his trouser pocket and dropped them onto the counter.

The shopkeeper scooped up the money then sidled past the old man and picked his way between the furniture to the shop window. He returned with the cane. The old man took hold of it.

"Should I wrap it?"

The old man did not answer. Instead, in his left hand he gripped the cane's centre then, with his right, twisted the end. The shopkeeper watched, astonished, as the handle turned and after four twists came away. The old man tossed the handle aside and turned the cane on its end. The expected contents did not tip onto the counter.

Nothing came out.

The old man lifted his head. The shopkeeper recoiled as sunken eyes peering out from the old man's cadaverous features fixed upon him. A

117

droplet of cold sweat dribbled down the fat man's spine. With the speed of a striking cobra an arm shot out and boney fingers grasped the shopkeeper's wrist. The old man moved closer, the ancient face now only centimeters away. A death mask.

"What the hell do you think you're doing? I'll call the police," the shop keeper muttered.

"Where is the rod?"

"I don't know anything about a rod."

The old man's eyes bored deep into the shopkeeper's soul.

"I believe you. Too bad."

Detective Daniel Vercoe squeezed past the uniformed officer in the doorway. He hung his umbrella on the back of an Elizabethan chair. Residual rain water dribbled onto what appeared to be an ancient Persian rug. Daniel considered himself an expert in antiquities. Over the years he had built up a modest collection and developed an eye that could distinguish between genuine and fake. The rug was genuine.

The thick-set detective in the dark suit scanned the premises until he picked out the coroner. Two men and a woman in white overalls carefully lifted tipped over oddments and dusted for fingerprints. Daniel circled the forensics team, zeroing in on the coroner kneeling beside the body.

"Do we know how he died yet, Doc?" Daniel asked, peering over the coroner's shoulder.

"Daniel. What took you so long? Don't tell me. Was she blonde, brunette or redhead?"

Daniel allowed a smile.

"All the above," he lied.

The coroner cut through the victim's shirt.

"Help me turn him."

Daniel bent and pulled on the fat shopkeeper's arm.

When the victim rolled onto his back, the coroner stood.

"Recognise him?"

Daniel shook his head.

"I think, even without an autopsy, I can pretty much tell you how he died. Beaten to death with this."

The coroner held up the cane. Daniel pulled on a pair of surgical gloves and took hold of it.

"A piece of wood. Heavy enough I suppose."

"To do this sort of damage to a body it needed strength. Your killer is strong."

"Anything else?"

"A Latin phrase is carved into the wood. "

Daniel studied the words. Frowned.

"What the hell does it say?"

"My medical school Latin is a little rusty but it pretty much says 'I am the bearer of life."

"Yeah, well, apart from the irony of this being the weapon of choice, I think we can dismiss it as a connection. Anything else?"

"Here on the floor. The victim has written a name in his own blood. Just like in the movies. See here: Rudiarius. Must be the killer's name. There you go Daniel. Half the job's done for you."

"Thanks Doc. I owe you one. I need to get back to the station. Catch you later."

Daniel parked in a no parking zone and put his police sign on the dash. Sometimes it worked. It was wet. The parking wardens would be drinking coffee and eating doughnuts. He rubbed his hand across stubble. He should have shaved.

"Daniel, meet your new partner, Lucinda Matters."

"I work alone, Chief, and you know why. No offence, Lucy, be grateful. "

"The name is Lucinda."

Daniel smiled. "Anything else, Lieutenant, I've got work to do?"

"I'm serious, Daniel. She works with you or you don't work. From the top. No arguments, it's a take it or leave it, and before you do anything stupid, like throw your badge at me, think it through. These are the new rules. Cops can't work alone anymore. The insurers don't like it and the captain don't like it, and internal affairs sure as hell don't like it."

Daniel turned and walked out of the room. Lucinda looked at the lieutenant. He gestured at her to follow.

Lucinda slid onto the vacant bar stool beside him.

"I'm having a beer. If you don't like it, leave."

"I'll have a beer."

Daniel waved to the barman and held up two fingers.

"Before you make a final decision directing your new career path as my partner, you need to be aware…"

"I've heard the rumours," Lucinda interrupted. "When I asked for a transfer my colleagues took great delight in informing me your nickname was DD, Detective Death. Three partners killed in as many years."

Daniel continued to stare into his beer but didn't touch it.

"I guess the question is, if you knew about me why go through with the transfer?"

"I want to be a detective. Becoming your partner is my only option." She raised her glass. "This will either be the beginning of a beautiful relationship or I become number four. Shit happens. We're cops. It goes with the territory. I need this and I won't let your paranoia fuck my career. So stop acting like an asshole. We're stuck with each other and I'm not taking a backward step because you've had a rotten life. Now are we or are we not going to investigate this murder?"

Daniel laughed. He took the glass from Lucinda's hand. "No drinking on duty. Barkeep, two coffees."

He glanced sideways at the crossed long legs. The navy gabardine had tightened round her thighs. She had a nice shape. He guessed she was thirty but looked younger. A pretty face, experienced. Her brunette hair cut short. For practical reasons, he guessed. An olive complexion meant she didn't need make-up. All the same, she did have a glow. A touch of rouge maybe.

"I've had a few thoughts," Lucinda started. "We should take the wooden cane to the university. A history professor. The Latin writing, the words might mean something. A special message."

"Don't waste your time. It was a second-hand shop. Our killer grabbed the closest piece of junk that would serve as a weapon, that's all. Knowing what an old carved message means won't help us one bit."

"I don't agree," Lucinda said. "The cane had an end removed."

"It broke off beating our victim to death," Daniel responded.

"No. I checked. The end screwed off. I screwed it back on again. The cane, rod, stick whatever you want to call it, was hollow. I think there was something inside or there was meant to be something inside. What if whoever killed our man unscrewed the top, didn't find what he was looking for and hit the victim over the head."

"Go to the top of the detective's class," Daniel said. "And what do you think might have been inside?"

"I don't know, but for such a brutal murder what could it be? Drugs? Cocaine? Diamonds?

Take your pick. What I do know is the top of that cane had been removed and placed on the counter top, and whoever removed it then killed the owner of the shop."

Daniel shrugged. A smirk across his face.

"Sneer all you like, I expect nothing less. You're a real bad ass. The talk is you should've been tossed off the force a long time ago. Just so you know. As a child I grew up in an abusive household, then when I married I spent two years with an asshole who beat me every time the weather turned shitty. When I joined the force the first thing I did was arrest the asshole. I rubbed his face into the bonnet of my car when I handcuffed him. So taking crap from another male who is fucked in the head doesn't faze me." She smiled.

Daniel held Lucinda's eye.

"Okay *Lucinda*, I apologise," Daniel said. "Where do you suppose we start?

"We have the killer's name: Rudiarius."

"I've run it already. Nothing came up."

Lucinda sipped her coffee. Daniel studied his new partner. She impressed him. He would need to keep an eye on Lucinda Matters.

"I'm going to the university. Are you coming?"

Daniel pushed his untouched coffee aside. "Lead the way."

The aged academic glanced over the top of his spectacles.

"Where did you get this?"

"It's a murder weapon," Daniel said. "We need to know if the words on this piece of wood have any special significance or whether it was just a handy implement of death."

"I do understand what it is you are asking of me, officer, but where did you find it?"

"In a junk shop."

"A curio shop," Lucinda corrected her partner. "Is this relevant?"

"Yes it is. If I'm right about what you have brought me then it had no place being anywhere other than in a museum."

Daniel remained passive but Lucinda's eyebrows arched. She gave Daniel a quick glance but he seemed disinterested. She, on the other hand, wanted to learn more.

"It's a piece of wood, Professor," Daniel said.

"No Detective, it might look like a piece of wood to you but I assure you it is a sword."

"A sword?' Lucinda asked. "It sure as hell doesn't look like one. And why a museum?"

"Because this is a Rudis. Old, not as old as it should be, and I would need to have it carbon dated, but all the same, I have seen a replica before, in Italy, and the one I saw looked like this but nowhere near as old."

"Just what is a Rudis?" Lucinda asked.

"The Rudis was a wooden sword used by Roman gladiators for training. This hard leather piece at the top that looks like a cut-in-half ball is

124

not adornment, it is a hand guard. The real significance of the Rudis was that when given to a gladiator as a gift, it signaled his freedom. It happened at the end of tournaments. The winner of all the fights might be awarded this, and some money if the Caesar felt so inclined. Or sometimes the slave owner - gladiators were slaves - might grant freedom. There was always a special ceremony when the Rudis was given. And, a special name was given to the freed gladiators."

"And what was that name, Professor?"

"Rudiarius."

Outside, Daniel shook his head in disbelief. Lucinda ignored him and checked her mobile. Melissa from forensics had left a message.

"This expert on ancient Rome the professor has suggested we talk to, I think we should go pay her a visit," Lucinda said.

Daniel shook his head.

"He said she's dotty and her mind wanders all over the place, plus she has all these loony theories about just about everything. It's a dead-end trail. Whatever happened two thousand years ago is not going to offer up any information we can use today, is it?"

"I would still like to talk to her."

"All right, but right now let's be good cops and follow the evidence. Let's go see Melissa."

###

As they entered Melissa's office, Daniel had convinced himself that his relationship with Lucinda would remain neutral, but when she reached across for the sugar bowl her perfume grabbed onto his senses like a piece of Velcro and dragged his thoughts into a place they had no right to go. He watched out the corner of his eye as she spooned a half measure of the white crystals into the mug of black coffee and stirred. She had lovely hands.

Melissa sat opposite placing photos on the table.

"We've had some luck. These are stills from the shop surveillance camera. The camera covered the door not the counter so we can't see the assault. The only customer, as far as we can tell, was an old man. It's not a great photo but clear enough to see that the old guy looks like he should be in a nursing home sucking soup through a straw and not wandering the streets beating people up. He looks harmless enough."

"So did the old ladies in *Arsenic and Old Lace*. I assume this is leading somewhere and you didn't just bring us in because we have an unclear photo of our killer?" Daniel asked.

Melissa shot him a glare that softened to a smile.

"Sorry. Stuck down here in the dungeons is lonely, no one to talk to. I have an assistant but he's not much of a conversationalist. Any chance I get to talk to a handsome detective I'll take and I am free for dinner."

"Melissa!" Daniel pleaded.

"Okay. Okay, I'll get to the point. My colleague does have a weakness: clothes. When he saw the coat the old gent was wearing he was adamant it did not come off the shelf. This guy is wearing top of the range gear. Very expensive. Tailor made. If you find the tailor you'll find the name of the man you're after. Of course, I can help you there."

"Really?" Daniel said, surprised." I never took you for someone who followed fashion."

"And just what is that supposed to mean? Are you sniping at my dress sense?"

"Of course not."

Melissa smiled. She turned to Lucinda, "They all back down in the end when you push back, Lucinda."

"Okay Melissa, how do you know the tailor?"

Melissa held up the coat. "It has a label."

Daniel insisted they split up. He had no desire to listen to the ravings of another academic and saw no value in pursuing information about Roman gladiators and ancient wooden swords. As she sat in a stifling sitting room, surrounded by cats and unclean dishes and the pungent smells of animal urine, Lucinda wished she had listened to Daniel and gone in search of the tailor.

Doctor Elizabeth Windsor sank into the leather chair close to the fire. Immediately two moggies leapt on her and fought for the privilege of sitting on her lap. She seemed not to notice. The old woman sipped her cold tea. Lucinda had declined the offer of refreshments when she saw milk from a cat's saucer added to the doctor's mug as whitening.

"You have a Rudis in your possession, my dear, interesting. It might be a replica but according to Professor Kingsman your Rudis is quite old and might be genuine. I think this unlikely."

"Why is that, Doctor?"

"To be authentic it would be close to two thousand years old and I would know about it. There are none. Not anywhere. No, it would be quite impossible for a Rudis to exist without my knowing. The only other explanation would be the myths. But they are nothing more than fairytales, made up by village storytellers"

"Humour me, Doctor. Any detail helps in the early stages of an investigation."

The doctor smiled. Lucinda saw her host's eyes sparkle and instincts told her she was about to be plunged into a mythology lesson.

"I've dedicated my life to investigating what I call the cold case legends of our past. We historians attempt to untangle truth from the interwoven fabric of facts and myth that makes up our history. Often we are successful. For example, the ancients believed that the mighty god Thor caused thunder. Modern science has proven this not to be true. Many myths and legends are just that - no more than fairy tales - but then there are other types. Conundrums in our past, puzzles not so black and white. These are the tiny threads of mystery I have followed but they are almost impossible to investigate, and alas, as yet most remain on my 'not-quite-proven' or 'disproved' lists."

"And one of your studies had something to do with this Rudis?"

"It had everything to do with the Rudis."

"What did you find out?" Lucinda asked when she met up with Daniel back at the bar. He nursed a coffee and Lucinda waved to the waiter to bring another.

"The tailor recognized the coat and I have a name."

"Well done. Do we share?"

"Jacob *Gibbs*," Daniel said.

"This name is meant to mean something to me?"

"It would if you read the business pages. Gibbs is the CEO and owner of Rolleston Pharmaceuticals."

"Holy shit," Lucinda said. She spooned some sugar into her coffee as she thought through the implications. "This is big. Do we take this to the lieutenant?"

"Not yet. All we have at the moment is a tailor telling us he made our suspect a coat. We need to talk to Mr Gibbs before we start throwing accusations about."

"Are you certain we should handle it this way? There is a procedure for high profile suspects. If we go behind the lieutenant's back and it turns nasty, he'll feed off our flesh for the rest of our careers."

"He'll be peeved, sure, but trust me, better an irate boss left out of the loop than an irate boss blasting us for making wild accusations, especially if you throw in this Roman sword stuff. He'll take your badge and send you to a hospital somewhere, and me as well for listening. Now come on. You wanted to be my partner, so be a partner."

Lucinda was hesitant. She would like to have argued the point but for once put her common sense to one side and agreed.

Jacob Gibbs lived on an estate on the outskirts of the city.

Daniel said he would drive them. It surprised Lucinda that he drove a BMW and not a gas guzzler.

"I like classic cars," Daniel explained. "Did the lady historian give you anything to work with?"

"She had a theory and I'm dreading telling it to you."

"It's a long drive. Humour will make it bearable."

"One of the freed slaves known as the Rudiarius, and this is from the doctor's own lips, was Spartacus. I'm sure you've heard of him."

Daniel nodded.

"I've seen the movie, Lucinda. The Romans captured and crucified him. He was never free."

"Our doctor tells a different story. She says that Spartacus was never captured. He and a few of his men made their way to Sicily. One moment," Lucinda pulled out her notebook and flicked the pages. "The Roman senate charged Marcus Crassus with ending the rebellion and he chased Spartacus and his men into southern Italy. Spartacus paid some pirates to transport him and a few of his men to Sicily. I looked this up on the web and it says that the pirates betrayed Spartacus and he never made it to Sicily, but our doctor is adamant he did. She says she has evidence. She also says that even Roman records show that when they defeated the rebels they never found the body of Spartacus. I checked this out too. And that is correct."

"And this has to do with us, how?" Daniel asked.

"This is where it gets weird."

"You mean it isn't weird enough already?" Daniel smiled.

"No laughing."

"Okay, out with it. I promise not to make faces."

There was gentleness to his tone and it surprised Lucinda.

131

"Our doctor spent many years in the Adriatic and lived in villages in Greece, Turkey, Sicily and southern Italy. No matter where she went in the region, she heard the same story from the old people. A legend passed down. It was her opinion that myths quite often proved to have substance and in this case there was no reason to believe otherwise."

"You're getting defensive. How far off the planet is this?" David asked.

"Out there with Jupiter, maybe further. The story goes that villagers returning from the markets after trading their year's harvest were set upon by bandits. The marauders had a reputation for ruthlessness and leaving no survivors. The villagers, incapable of defending themselves, believed all was lost. Then, a miracle: Spartacus and his men swept down from the hills and, although outnumbered, had superior fighting skills and killed the cutthroats. Back in the village grateful elders welcomed Spartacus and his men with a special feast and called forth the sorceress Drusilla. Drusilla had great powers and spoke directly to the gods."

"Bloody hell, Lucinda," Daniel laughed, "you have got to be joking."

"The villagers had come to Sicily from Crete and brought with them the spirit of a powerful god, Dionysos. That night Drusilla called to the great god and asked for a special reward for

Spartacus and his men. Dionysos was the god who guarded the gates between life and death."

Daniel shook his head again, still laughing.

Lucinda took a deep breath and held her composure.

"That night Dionysos reached into the smoking volcano of Mount Vesuvius and pulled out molten lava and forged it into ten rods. These she gave to Spartacus and his men, and as long as they possessed them the rods would guarantee them eternal life."

"Hold on. Now, you are not going to say what I think you are going to say. That these rods are kept in a Rudis and that these guys are alive today?"

Lucinda gave Daniel a playful push.

"I'm telling you what she told me."

"And did this woman live with a lot of cats?"

Lucinda chose not to answer.

Daniel passed a line of cars parked on the grass verge.

"Mr Gibbs has visitors," Lucinda said.

"Look at the size of his house. It's big enough to be a hotel."

Daniel found a space and pulled over.

"How do we handle this?" Lucinda asked.

"Let's get him separated from his guests and have a chat to begin with. Spot the body language, that sort of shit. If he lies, like denying he was even there, then we will take him in."

The two detectives stood on the granite-paved terracing and Daniel pushed an intercom button. Lucinda looked up at the second storey. She saw no lights on. After a few minutes Daniel pushed the button again.

"You'd think he'd have a butler of some sort," Lucinda said.

Daniel tried the door. It opened.

"We need a warrant."

"I hear suspicious sounds from within. You hear it, partner?"

She rolled her eyes. "I hear it."

"Good." Daniel stepped inside. "Jesus. This foyer is the size of my apartment. Look at all the artwork! The place looks like a room at the Louvre."

Lucinda walked up to a painting and squinted at the signature. "It must be a copy."

Daniel shrugged. "He's a wealthy man."

She followed Daniel down the corridor.

The door ahead was ajar and light gleamed into the darkened hallway. Lucinda felt for her pistol. Daniel looked back at her. She nodded she was ready. He pushed the door open and they entered. He stopped after two paces. Lucinda looked over his shoulder.

"Mother of God."

The coat on the crumpled life-form in the leather chair was identical to that worn by the man in the curio shop. Inside the clothes a body, and the skin had sunk into the bones.

"It looks as if all fluid has been sucked from the corpse," Lucinda said, taking a tissue from her purse and holding it over her nose, "This is not normal, Daniel. Gibbs did not look like that two days ago."

"No, he did not."

Lucinda moved across to the writing desk in the corner, sheets of paper strewn across it. Lucinda picked up a sheet. It listed corporations. She studied the names for a few minutes then she called to Daniel.

"You're not going to believe this."

He joined her at the table and took the paper from her.

"It's a list of companies."

Daniel said, "Gibbs was a business man. These are probably companies he was dealing with."

"Look closer."

"What am I looking for?"

"The names, Utility Broking, Akron Holdings….."

"I can read, Lucinda," Daniel interrupted.

"There are eight names on that list and if you add Gibbs's company, Rolleston Pharmaceuticals, the first letters of each company spell Rudiarius."

"Now you have gone batty."

"I don't believe in coincidences, Daniel."

"Listen to what you're saying, Lucinda, and think. Do you really want to take this to the captain? A fairytale story of Spartacus and his men having eternal life and that they have all lived into our lifetime and built these companies so they can control the world or whatever. And that poor old Gibbs here, lost his rod of life and has had a meltdown but the others are still out there?"

"When you put it like that it does sound crazy," Lucinda said.

"You put it like that, not me. Please don't mention my name. Look there will be a logical explanation for all this. It could be one of those super bugs they have in the hospitals these days that killed Gibbs."

"Okay, okay, but what about the visitors? Where are they?"

"Maybe the cars belong to Gibbs?"

"You know that's not likely. The cars look newly parked. I doubt Gibbs could drive them all."

"Okay, good point. Come on, let's go find these people."

"Where?"

"It's a big house. Don't you go to the movies? Big houses always have a dungeon."

"What about backup?"

"Why? To surround our decomposing killer?"

"Smart ass."

Daniel said, "Look, Gibbs has a rotting body but you saw for yourself there is no evidence of foul play, is there? If there are people here they might be holding a meeting of some sort that doesn't involve Gibbs. Maybe a management get-together and no one has noticed their boss is dead. Let's find them and ask some questions. I can't call out the SWAT team because maybe someone is here but we aren't sure, and gee whiz, they might be trouble but there is no evidence they will be. "

"All right, all right, I get it," Lucinda said.

"Come on, let's go find them."

The stairwell was easy enough to find, and as Lucinda descended closely behind Daniel she heard voices. At the end of a long narrow passageway an open door emitted light: the voices came from within. Lucinda remained apprehensive. She tapped Daniel on the shoulder.

"Are you sure we should be doing this? What if they're armed? No one even knows where we are."

Daniel turned to face her.

"Lucinda, there is no crime. Not yet. Gibbs just died. Weirdly, I'll concede, but there could be any number of explanations." Lucinda's eyebrows arched. "Well okay, not any number but an explanation other than murder. Whoever is in that room was not with Gibbs in the curio shop. It might be servant's quarters for all we know. Right now we are just making enquiries, nothing more."

Lucinda shook her head. "You keep saying there is no crime. Until forensics say Gibbs wasn't murdered, we can't rule it out. Just because it doesn't look like a crime scene it can't be ruled out."

"Okay, okay, but we're here now. I'm going in. Are you my partner or not?"

Lucinda nodded. She knew Daniel was right but the further down the corridor they walked, the more claustrophobic she became and that made her nervous. It was like walking down a mine shaft, and like a mine shaft there was only way out and that was now a long way behind them.

Daniel pushed the steel door aside and the noises grew louder. They slipped through then the door, on a spring, closed behind them. Lucinda stared at the door. She turned to Daniel but he had moved on, so she had little choice but to follow. They went through another door into a room as sizable as the entry foyer.

Eight men sat round a long table. There were two empty chairs.

When they saw Daniel the men stood and chanted, "Spartacus! Spartacus! Spartacus!"

Lucinda's mouth dropped as confusion and realization dawned. She studied him closer: the black hair, olive complexion, steely eyes and Roman nose. She had met enough Italian men. Daniel had the look.

Daniel turned to her. "It really is too bad you are such a good detective. As you can see, we are in a chamber deep beneath the earth. It was built centuries ago and is known only to we few."

Lucinda glanced at the empty chair. Daniel followed her gaze and answered her unasked question.

"Gibbs was becoming too showy, endangering our group. I cast him out two years ago which is why he had aged so much. The curio shop owner was the go-between. I paid him to place the Rudis in the window. Gibbs was given the address and a time to collect. If he found the rod in the sword then he was welcome back into the fold. I decided that forgiveness could not be granted. You know the rest of the story."

Daniel turned his attention back to the men standing round the table.

Daniel took his place at the head of the table. He fixed his eyes on the group then nodded. Each man produced a key and plunged it into the hole in front of them, another nod and they turned the keys ninety degrees, there was an audible click. A section of the table top slid back. Daniel reached forward and pulled out the wooden swords and passed a Rudis to each man.

"We were lucky this time," he said. Each man began to unscrew the handle from the swords. "We must remain vigilant."

"But you're a cop," Lucinda blurted out.

"I am a sentinel, Lucinda. Knowing what the law is up to is our protection from it."

With the handles screwed off, Daniel and the men upturned the blades and glass-like rods fell into their hands. They placed the rods upright into the holes in the table. Daniel read out loud the words on the wooden blade.

"I am the bearer of life."

The men repeated the mantra in chorus.

Within seconds the rods of Dionysos began to glow.

The men breathed in the radiating life.

For another year, youth restored.

Lucinda turned and rushed to the door. Desperate, she pushed against the steel barrier but it was hopeless. The locking mechanism had already slid into place.

THE END

www.thomasryanwriter.com

Short Stories (Volume 1)

Ryan's short stories span the spectrum of human emotions, from the creepy 'Nightmares', to the fun and humour of 'The World's Biggest Bun'. Ryan believes all good short stories should have unexpected twists and turns. Applying his thriller techniques he manages to achieve this end. Readers will find Ryan's short story writing gripping and easy to read.

Quoting a reviewer, 'these are very intriguing, original stories, all well written and enjoyable. Ryan really gets inside his characters and makes their world our world, whatever its moral code or unwritten rules. These stories are powerful and stay with you once you've finished them.'

Thomas Ryan constructs seven perfectly paced capsules of fiction.' Red City Review

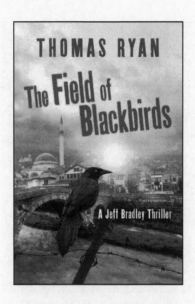

Former SAS soldier Jeff Bradley thought he had left warzones behind when he inherited a vineyard in rural New Zealand. But now his vineyard manager, Arben Shala, has gone missing in his native Kosovo. An enigmatic message tells Jeff that his friend is in grave danger.

Determined to find Arben and bring him home, Jeff travels to Kosovo and finds a lawless state in the grip of criminal gangs. Corrupt officials obscure every lead. With the help of USAID director Morgan Delaney, Jeff delves into the province's seedy underworld and uncovers a conspiracy of terrifying scale. A web of dark connections links the captors with a terrorist bombing campaign across Europe, and now it is no longer just Arben whose survival is at stake.

Double-crossed by allies, watched at every turn, can Jeff get to the heart of the conflict before the warlords get to him?

14611139R00088

Printed in Great Britain
by Amazon.co.uk, Ltd.,
Marston Gate.